"Alexandra? What are you doing here?"

Clearly Fletcher regarded her as an intruder. How could this happen? He had come to the city and made exquisite love to her and changed her life forever. "You're surprised to see me," Ally whispered.

"Surprise is one word I could choose, I guess," Fletcher drawled, his deep voice rumbling with sarcasm. His eyes traveled—very deliberately—over her slim frame. "What are you doing here?" he repeated, his voice less harsh this time, as if he had run out of breath suddenly.

"I have brought your little godson, Connor. You're his guardian now...."

"I know damn well I'm his guardian, but what have you got to do with it?"

"Well, the point is," resumed Ally, "I'm his nanny."

The color in Fletcher's face deepened while, with the worst sense of timing, a kookaburra broke into raucous laughter in a gum tree overhanging the track. "Ally! You can't be!"

CB   Br

Barbara Hannay was born in Sydney, educated in Brisbane and has spent most of her adult life living in tropical North Queensland, where she and her husband have raised four children. While she has enjoyed many happy times camping and canoeing in the Australian bush, she also delights in an urban life-style—chamber music, contemporary dance, movies and dining out. An English teacher, she has always loved writing and now, by having her stories published, she is living her most cherished fantasy.

Outback Wife and Mother is Barbara's outstanding debut title for Harlequin Romance®—we just know you'll love her heartwarming style, so look out for more from her in the future!

Outback Wife and Mother
Barbara Hannay

HARLEQUIN®

TORONTO • NEW YORK • LONDON
AMSTERDAM • PARIS • SYDNEY • HAMBURG
STOCKHOLM • ATHENS • TOKYO • MILAN • MADRID
PRAGUE • WARSAW • BUDAPEST • AUCKLAND

For John Dow,
who was my father and my first hero

ISBN 0-373-03578-0

OUTBACK WIFE AND MOTHER

First North American Publication 1999.

Copyright © 1999 by Barbara Hannay.

PROLOGUE

MUMMY was crying again.

Lying in his bed, the boy could hear her muffled sobs and his father's pleading voice in the next room. 'But, Vivienne, you mustn't go. You can't leave us.'

He could see the friendly silhouette of his teddy bear on the pillow beside him, but not even his favourite toy could help him feel safe or happy. Not when he could hear the desperate sadness in his mother's voice.

'I feel so—so stifled here in the outback,' she sobbed. 'I think I'll go mad.'

Eventually, he pulled the pillow over his head to shut out the frightening voices...

Then with the first creamy fingers of dawn, his mother crept into the room, smelling as fresh as flowers. She sat on the edge of his bed and he buried his head in her lap.

'Mon petit,' she whispered, stroking his hair. 'I will miss you so much.'

Something started to thump loudly in his chest. 'You don't have to miss me, Mummy,' he cried. 'I'm going to stay on Wallaroo with you and Daddy for always.'

With a choked moan, she hugged him close, cradling him with her soft, warm arms. 'Oh, cheri,' she whispered and, looking up, he saw her beautiful eyes fill with bright tears. 'Always remember, I love you very, very much. But you belong here.'

There was a crunch of tyres on gravel in the yard outside, and then heavy footsteps on the wooden floorboards of the veranda. Ned, the stockman, stood in the doorway.

He cleared his throat as he fiddled with his wide-brimmed hat.

'Yes, Ned. I'm coming,' she said softly.

The boy felt her warm lips on his cheek and she held him so tightly he couldn't breathe. Then she stood up and drifted away from him, out of the room, as soft and pretty as the morning mist on the river.

His feet hit the cold floor as he hurried after her.

Outside, the bush was already waking. A huge flock of pink and grey galahs rose from the gum trees along the creek, filling the reddening sky with their raucous chorus. Ned opened the door to the truck and she slipped inside. The little boy could just make out her pale face through the window glass.

He ran faster, but as he reached the top of the steps, two strong arms caught him and lifted him up and he felt his father's bristly morning cheek pressed against his. 'We've got to let her go, Fletcher,' he said, his voice sounding gruff and strange. 'She doesn't belong in the bush. She needs the city lights.'

What was Daddy talking about? Of course Mummy belonged here. The truck's engine spluttered to life and the station dogs barked and yapped at its tyres.

'It's just you and me now, little mate. At least she let me have you…'

The truck rolled forward.

Thoroughly bewildered now, the boy struggled in his father's arms and cried out to her, 'Mummy, don't go!'

But the truck gathered speed. And she looked back at him one last time, raised a graceful hand to her lips and blew him a kiss.

CHAPTER ONE

FLETCHER HARDY ran an irritated finger around the inside of his uncomfortably stiff collar and glared at the marbled floors and mirrored walls of the enormous ballroom. He had rushed straight to the hotel from a press conference about the drought in North Queensland and he had to postpone a dinner meeting with the Minister for Primary Industries—simply to watch half-starved girls sashaying around in outrageous costumes!

He prided himself on never doing anything against his will, but in a rare moment of weakness he had allowed his cousin, Lucette, to talk him into coming to a fashion show.

Grimacing as his shoulders met the unfamiliar constraints of his tux, he strode impatiently towards the rows of seats arranged around the catwalk. He ignored the swing of expensively coiffed female heads trailing after him like sunflowers following the sun.

And he scowled as he found his seat and lowered his long body into it.

Fashion! Ridiculous female obsession, he'd always claimed, happily overlooking the minor detail that he had, on odd occasions in the past, been known to admire an elegantly designed garment gracing a beautiful woman.

As soon as Lucette had heard Fletcher was travelling south to Melbourne, she'd begged him to come and watch the show so he could admire the set she designed especially for this exhibition. He'd found his kid cousin's enormous pride in her first real assignment quite touching and so, to humour her, he had come. But where was she now? The live band was blasting out its opening number and the lights were going down and still no Lucette! She'd left him to brave this torment on his own!

Typical. With any luck there would be an interval and he could leave.

Wrapped in these angry thoughts, he refused to join in the applause as the grinning compere, dressed in a gold tuxedo, approached the microphone, welcomed the audience and delivered a totally incomprehensible joke about fashion. The audience roared. Fletcher growled.

'This evening, the Quintessential Collection brings us a preview of the new season highlights from five of Australia's top young designers. We begin with the delightful Alexandra Fraser. I'm sure most of the menfolk here would agree with me, that Ally is herself rather beautifully designed...' Here the compere paused for a brief titter from the audience, while Fletcher almost groaned aloud. 'Today we see fine examples of her ultra-urban, minimalist designs in pale cashmeres and silks,' the compere continued with a wide, plastic smile. 'And you should note the clever addition of silk cummerbunds to her slinky pants and long evening skirts.'

Fletcher raked a hand distractedly through his thick, dark hair as, for the sake of his sanity, he turned his attention to Lucette's set. OK, it was good. Against an ethereal backdrop resembling the sky at dawn—all pinks and golds—there were delicate, gilded arches encrusted with winking bud lights and a runway edged with more tiny lights and misty clumps of tulle. It all seemed appropriate, he decided, suggesting a show, which would present the quintessence of earthly beauty. And as far as he could see the decor provided a suitable accompaniment for the palely elegant fashions, which soon emerged.

But as for the deportment and grace of the models slinking and strutting along the runway—he barely noticed them. His eyes were squinted with his efforts to read his watch in the darkened room. But his attempts were futile so instead he began scanning the audience, searching for Lucette. After several fruitless minutes, he tried the watch again. No use. When could he safely slip away?

Restlessly, he squirmed in his seat. His elbow bumped the thin woman sitting beside him and she glowered at him from beneath her wide-brimmed hat.

About to scowl back at her, his attention was suddenly captured by a woman emerging down the runway. Dressed in the simplest of short gowns in deep purple, the colour of crushed violets, she stood out in stark contrast to the whites, creams and beiges worn by the models surrounding her.

'Ladies and gentleman, our very own Alexandra Fraser.'

So this was the designer of the first collection. She was bowing as the crowd applauded her. Cries of 'Bravo' could even be heard, so obviously she was being well received.

She smiled out into the audience and at that precise moment, the simple, two syllable word *woman* took on an entirely new level of meaning for Fletcher Hardy.

This woman was like no other he'd ever seen before. An unnerving tension seized his body. His hands gripped the upholstered arms of his seat and incredibly, this hardened man of the land's throat tightened over a huge lump of unexpected emotion as his gaze remained transfixed by the figure on the catwalk.

She was surrounded by tall, willowy models, but his eyes were drawn from their almost asexual leanness to her startling femininity. Her gleaming dark hair and pale skin were a perfect foil for the rich colour of her one-shoulder dress and the delectable curves it barely concealed. Her slender legs and the graceful movement of her dainty hands as she acknowledged the models were utterly fascinating. Spellbound, he watched this dark-haired, enchanting designer.

She was the most exquisite female he had ever seen.

Her features were delicate yet determined and her thickly lashed grey eyes sparkled with intelligence and spunk. Surrounded as she was by models looking as vacant as dolls in a shop window, this woman looked vibrant, incredibly alive, undeniably sexy.

And then she was gone, tossing a final smile over her one bared shoulder before disappearing with the models back through Lucette's golden arches.

Another group of models bounced onto the runway accompanied by wild heavy metal music. Fletcher had a vague impression of a kaleidoscopic mix of lace and satin teamed with psychedelic stockings and electric blue lips, but his mind was still totally absorbed by Alexandra Fraser. If only he had bothered to pick up a catalogue on his way in, he might have discovered more about her.

Restlessly he sat through the gyrations and outlandish creations of the second collection but as soon as its designer, a young man whose bald head was wildly tattooed, appeared to receive his applause, Fletcher rose from his seat and made his way quickly to the back of the ballroom.

He found a stack of catalogues on a small side table and hurriedly snatched one up, leafing through it impatiently. Reading by the light of a dimmed wall lamp, he found little to satisfy him. There was a brief description of Alexandra Fraser's collection and a list of several awards she had won and then a quoted comment.

'Alexandra says of fashion design, "I keep to simple

lines, neat silhouettes, no frills or fluffiness, but this doesn't mean my clothes cannot be soft or reveal the body. For me design is a passionate experience. It fulfils me totally—mind, body and soul.''''

To his annoyance Fletcher Hardy did not find the scraps of information at all comforting and he skulked around the back of the ballroom as the show continued, feeling startled and miserable. How could fashion fulfil such a beautiful woman?

And he knew then that, after the show, his next move would be to dismiss the waiting limousine, courtesy of the Cattlemen's Union.

And then he would be heading backstage.

Ally Fraser made her excited way through the backstage confusion. Around her, models were changing, some removing wigs or false eyelashes, while assistants gathered up costumes and shoes. As she passed, nearly everyone looked up to smile or to openly congratulate her. She was trying not to grin too widely, but her collection had clearly drawn the most enthusiastic audience response of the entire Quintessential show and she was over the moon. More importantly, she'd noticed at least two fashion journalists nodding and smiling at her when she'd taken her bow.

She stopped to check that several of her garments were being stored away properly and thought fleetingly of how wonderful it would be to be able to head straight for home and an early night. But although she was dead tired after the hectic pace of the past few weeks, she steeled herself to go outside to join in the cocktails and to be particularly pleasant to the fashion editors.

Quickly she glanced around the crowded room, making sure everything was under control before she left.

However there was a rather uncontrolled and excited

babble erupting from the models in the far corner as a strange man walked into their midst. Ally stared, intrigued. These girls were so used to having all kinds of people wander in and out of their changing areas that they usually took no notice. But they were paying a great deal of attention to this good-looking stranger.

To her surprise, Ally saw that he was ignoring the girls' varied stages of undress as he advanced purposefully across the room. Most newcomers, especially males, couldn't keep their eyes from straying frantically. To her even greater surprise, she realised that the tall, dark intruder appeared to be heading straight for her. In his sleek, black tux, marching head and shoulders above the models, he advanced, staring at her so intently she felt her pulses begin to race.

'I'm looking for Lucette Hardy,' he said, as soon as he reached her.

His voice was deep and resonant and his claim sounded quite plausible and yet Ally found that she couldn't believe him. She had never considered herself to have telepathic insight, but this man's eyes were so fiercely fixed on hers that she knew straight away that he was seeking her out. And the knowledge held her, standing before him, mesmerised by his height, his strong, handsome face and his piercing blue eyes which looked exactly as if they had been made from summer skies.

As those eyes continued to explore every detail of her face, she struggled to speak. 'Poor Lucette's come down with flu,' she said. 'She's devastated to miss the show.'

'So that's what happened.' He looked away briefly and then his eyes found hers once again. 'You are—' he began and then cleared his throat as he corrected himself. 'Your designs are absolutely exquisite.' With a sweeping gesture, he indicated the racks of her clothes. 'The simple lines...' He paused, apparently lost for words.

'And neat silhouettes?' she supplied, her lips curled in sudden amusement.

He grinned then, a cheeky grin that totally transformed his face. 'OK, I read your comments in the catalogue. But honestly, I like the dress you're wearing best of all.'

'Thank you,' she replied. It was certainly not the first time she had received a compliment, but most of the praise that came her way was delivered with such a practised smoothness that it smacked of insincerity and slipped over her like an old, warm blanket that she took for granted. This evening her heart pounded erratically in response to his clumsy admission and she stared back at the sun-tanned, ruggedly handsome face knowing that she had never met a man like him. In contrast to her world of image-makers and haute couture, his masculinity seemed to be stripped of all pretension.

He frowned and she was surprised at the way his gaze dropped to his work-toughened hands as if he were suddenly shy. With a totally unexpected jolt of disappointment, she thought, soon he'll say it was a pleasure to meet me and then he'll be gone.

In the awkward silence, she looked back at him, taking in his broad shoulders, thick, black hair, rugged features and vivid blue eyes and wondered how someone who embodied the fantasies of half the women on the planet could make such a hash of what was clearly meant to be a simple pick-up.

'We haven't really met you know,' she heard herself saying a little too eagerly. 'You haven't even told me your name.'

He grinned again and visibly relaxed, his strong features turning so sunny that for a moment Ally thought the technical crew were playing tricks with the lighting.

'I'm Fletcher Hardy, Lucette's cousin. In Melbourne on business. I actually came to admire Lucette's work.'

She half expected him to trot out something trite about ending up admiring the designer instead, but to her relief he didn't. Instead he asked, 'When do you finish here?'

'I'm afraid I've got to do my duty out there first.' She grimaced, pointing to the ballroom. 'Meet the press, that sort of thing.'

He pulled a face. 'You have my sympathy. I've had a day of that sort of thing myself.'

'Really?' She looked at Fletcher Hardy contemplatively. 'Now let me guess. You do something in the outdoors. A ski instructor? No, the press wouldn't bother you about that. Perhaps a mountaineer? Are you about to conquer something generally considered unconquerable?'

Fletcher laughed, throwing back his head and drawing sharp glances from others in the room, then he looked her over slowly and said softly and with wicked audacity, 'I'd say I might be in with a chance.'

The ripple of excitement that raced up her spine shocked Ally. This cousin of Lucette's was losing his shyness with breathtaking speed.

'I never was much good at guessing games,' she said quickly to cover her sudden self-consciousness. But she didn't mind his cheek. She'd never before felt such an immediate connection with another person, especially a man. No one else, on first meeting, had accelerated her heartbeat to such a heady, scampering pace. 'You'll have to remain a mystery for now,' she added. 'I really must go to this party. Why don't you join us?'

'Sure. Lead the way.'

Ally was aware of many eyes watching as Fletcher followed her into the cocktail party. As they helped themselves to champagne cocktails, Derek Squires, the bald-headed, much-tattooed designer rushed over to them.

'Darlings,' he crooned.

'Hello, Derek. I'd like you to meet Fletcher Hardy.'

'And hello-o, darling,' smiled Derek, eyeing Fletcher with open interest. Fletcher nodded politely.

'How's it all going?' Ally asked.

'Just keep me away from that dreadful woman,' shuddered Derek.

'Who's that?'

'Phoebe Hardcastle. She had the cheek to criticise my lovely blue lipstick. Said my girls looked half drowned.' He trembled in horror. 'She has the creative imagination of a fruit fly.'

'She certainly can be very cutting,' agreed Ally, flashing a quick glance at Fletcher to see how he was reacting to the conversation. His eyes were wide with interest.

'She has no understanding of fashion flair. Stupid cow.'

'Now let's not get too critical of cows,' cut in Fletcher. 'They're my stock-in-trade.' Both Derek and Ally looked at him curiously, waiting for more explanation. 'I raise cattle,' he said with a shrug.

'Oh, how awful for you,' murmured Derek, backing off hurriedly.

Ally smiled, her grey eyes dancing as she looked up at Fletcher from under her thick, dark lashes. 'I knew you did something in the outdoors.'

'Ally Fraser,' boomed a commanding voice from behind them. 'Spare me a minute or two if you please.'

An alarming-looking woman with bright red hair, thick spectacles and a heavy jaw pushed her way next to Ally.

'Oh, Phoebe. How are you this evening?'

'Tolerable, dear. But I've deadlines to meet. Can you answer a couple of quick questions?'

Ally shot Fletcher a swift, mildly apologetic glance and nodded. 'Fire away.'

'What I want, darling,' the redhead began, shoving a small tape recorder under Ally's nose, 'is for you to sum up in a nutshell…who you're trying to appeal to…who you expect to wear your clothes…who is going to connect with them.'

'But I've told you all that many times,' Ally protested.

'New show, new comments,' the journalist shot back, her eyes hard and unsympathetic.'

'Very well,' replied Ally after only a moment's hesitation. 'I think my clients are people who are looking for value…for something contemporary, but with classical elegance as well…'

She felt a strong hand pat her heartily on the back and looked up to catch Fletcher winking at her.

There were more questions which Ally answered as best she could, but the whole time she was terribly conscious of the way Fletcher's hand stayed there, resting on her bare shoulder. Her skin beneath the warm hand tingled deliciously in response.

'And are you planning to launch a range of perfumes, like some of the other more successful designers?' Phoebe was asking.

Ally wavered. This was something she had been considering, but it was too soon to talk about it.

'Good question,' cut in Fletcher. 'And when we have the answer to that, you'll be the first to know. We'll give you an exclusive, but for now we have another engagement.'

'Who are you?' spluttered Phoebe, looking up at Fletcher, her red-painted mouth agape.

'I'm Ms. Fraser's public relations consultant. It was very nice of you to give us your attention, but I'm afraid that's all we have time for.'

Ally gave a startled gasp, but the hand on her shoulder remained firmly in place as she felt herself gently but purposefully led away.

'What do you think you're doing?' she cried, twisting around to face him.

'Ssh. I'll explain in a minute.'

Frowning, and with lips pursed, Ally walked quietly beside Fletcher until they made their way through the throng and reached the main door of the ballroom.

'OK, now tell me what you're doing,' she demanded, still frowning and with her arms crossed over her chest.

'I'm abducting you,' he said quietly.

Then as she opened her mouth to retaliate, Fletcher placed a finger over her lips. 'I'm taking you away, because you're the most intriguing woman I've ever seen and I don't have much time in Melbourne and...we don't have time for all the social niceties.'

They stood staring at one another, his finger still warm on her lips. Ally was stunned.

'But my career hangs on these interviews,' she stammered.

'Do you really think so?'

She hesitated. It was a question she'd asked herself many times. She had always tried to 'do the right thing.' It was the way she'd been brought up, but she knew that little of what she'd actually said to a journalist ever appeared in print and usually when it did, she was furious at being misquoted.

Fletcher continued. 'These journos have already made their notes and taken their photographs. And they've already made up their minds about your clothes. Now all they want is free food and grog, to be seen with celebrities and to catch up on the hot gossip.'

Ally suspected that he was right. And, she reflected, she'd placed work before pleasure for so long now that she could hardly remember the last time she'd given in to capricious self-indulgence. If she hadn't been so certain this man was going to be incredibly important to her, she might have wavered. But her mind was too distracted by the thrill of intense excitement and heady anticipation she'd felt from the moment she first saw him. And that simple touch of his hand on her shoulder had seduced her body more surely than the most concerted efforts of any of her previous admirers. She could have been making the biggest mistake of her life, but suddenly she didn't care. Being with Fletcher Hardy became the only possible option.

'Where would you like to go?' she asked with a smile.

'Do you like Thai food?'

'Love it.'

They took a taxi to the best Thai restaurant in the city.

'You know Melbourne well?' Ally asked as their taxi wove through the traffic.

'Only the inner city area. I usually only come down for conferences once or twice a year.'

'And these cows of yours. Beef or dairy?'

'Beef. I own a cattle property on the Burdekin River. Wallaroo Downs.'

'The Burdekin? That's in North Queensland, isn't it?'

'Sure is.'

'A long way from here.' Ally tried not to sound too bothered by this news.

'About three thousand kilometres.'

'And you like living up there?'

'Yes. I do.' He slanted her a slow smile and stretched his arm along the back of the seat. 'And I like visiting down here.'

The restaurant was fairly crowded, but there were still some tables to spare. The gleaming timber furniture, soft cream wool carpeting and enormous ceramic urns of beautiful fresh flowers provided a formal enough atmosphere for them to feel at ease in their elegant evening wear.

'It's been too long since I dined out,' Fletcher commented after they were seated.

'Well, at least you have an excuse,' said Ally. 'I don't suppose there are too many restaurants on your block, but I'm surrounded by them and I still don't indulge much.'

'So, tonight is a treat for both of us,' smiled Fletcher, and Ally wondered if she had ever seen quite such a sexy smile.

It was ridiculous to feel so excited, so expectant, as if she were a child on her birthday surrounded by beautifully tempting, as-yet-unopened presents, or a skydiver on the brink of a thrilling leap into the unknown.

She willed her stomach to stop fluttering as they chatted about the menu, discussed the food and wine, their likes and dislikes. When the waiter came, Fletcher pronounced the Thai dishes with surprising fluency.

'You've been to Thailand?' she asked.

'Not as a tourist. Strictly business.'

'But you took time out for the important business of eating.'

Fletcher grinned and reached out to take her hand. 'I'm rather glad Lucette harangued me into coming to your show.' He looked down at her hand, which seemed so small and white in his sun-tanned grasp. 'No rings,' he said and then added with a lift of one dark eyebrow, 'Does that also mean no strings?'

'My work pulls me in all kinds of directions,' Ally admitted. 'But no strings of the personal variety. I've been rather single-minded about focusing on my career.'

'I can't believe there haven't been numerous attempts to sidetrack you.'

She tasted the crisp, white wine Fletcher had chosen while she considered his comment.

'A girl has to be careful.' She looked straight into his

bright blue eyes. 'There have been plenty of wolves in the forest, but I always thought Little Red Riding Hood was far too easily led. I've mostly ignored them and just kept on going, heading straight for Granny's house.'

'In this case, Granny's house being the Quintessential label?'

'Yes.' She smiled.

'So, after the resounding success of this evening's show, perhaps you've earned yourself a little diversion,' he said.

'Per-perhaps.'

But, just remember, a warning voice sounded in her head, that is all this man who lives three states away can possibly be—a temporary diversion. A pleasant—an extremely pleasant—dinner companion.

The meal was superb. A delicious soup of seafood simmered in coconut milk, ginger and coriander was followed by special Thai curries—a green beef curry for Fletcher and a red chicken version for Ally. Both dishes were accompanied by aromatic spoonfuls of fluffy, jasmine rice.

For Ally, the meal, the wine and the accompanying conversation were highly charged. While no one else had ever made her feel so comfortable, her bubbling emotions continually kept her on edge—incredibly excited and happier than she could ever remember, but nervous, too, wondering what on earth she would do when this meal was over and it was time for them to go their separate ways.

They talked and laughed together and she found herself telling Fletcher more about her love for fashion and her ambitions, and he listened intently, making her feel that she was a fascinating conversationalist. He talked a little about the conference that had brought him to Melbourne and very briefly about Wallaroo Downs.

Throughout the meal, his eyes were watching her. They seemed to travel restlessly from her face and throat to her arms and back again and she knew he was as sensitive as she was to something intensely strong and powerful filling the space between them. It was a heady, almost suffocating tension. This must be what they call sexual chemistry, Ally thought with bewildered fascination. Until now men had only ever induced in her a kind of bemused, gentle stirring of her senses. But Fletcher's compelling masculinity triggered an elemental need that startled her.

So that when they left the restaurant and stepped out onto the street, Ally found herself turning to Fletcher and saying a trifle nervously, 'My apartment's only two blocks away. We could walk there if you like—for coffee.'

'Great idea,' he said with an easy smile and took her hand as they set off.

You've only just met the man, Ally kept reminding herself as they passed late-night coffee shops and silent, darkened office buildings. So, your hormones have come out of hibernation, but just remember you never, ever sleep with anyone on a first date.

'How long are you in town for?' she surprised herself by asking. It was a question she'd avoided all evening.

'Three days.'

Only three days! 'Oh.' Ally bit down hard on her lip, but it was too late to stifle the cry of disappointment.

Perhaps Fletcher shared her reaction, for he paused and, drawing her into the shadows of a shopfront, gathered her closer to him.

'And that reminds me...' he murmured.

'Reminds you?' Ally's voice trembled, her breath snatched away by his proximity. Up so close, she could feel his warm breath on her cheek, sense the strong muscles beneath his suit jacket and smell the spicy tang of his aftershave. In the scant light thrown by a street lamp some distance away, she could see his delicious smile. His eyes held hers and as she looked into the blue depths, she knew she had never wanted to be kissed more than she did now.

If only he needed to kiss her as much as she needed to taste his beautiful, sensuous mouth. Her ears buzzed, her heart had surely stopped beating. Was she breathing? Everything seemed to have stopped.

'I'm reminded,' he whispered, 'that it's time to start kissing you now. We really don't have time to waste, do we?' His hand cradled her cheek. 'I've been wanting to kiss you all evening,' he said. Then he lowered his lips to hers, to take her mouth gently in a kiss so tender, so tempting, that it only served to fire a desperate longing for more. Her lips parted eagerly as his mouth met hers again, to kiss her more deeply, more urgently, his arms binding her hard against him.

Ally hardly knew how to cope with the jolt of wild sensations that surged through her.

'O-oh,' she moaned softly, wondering if her feet still touched the ground, knowing at once that she belonged in this man's arms. Not wanting his mouth to ever leave hers. Nothing had ever felt so right.

He broke away as footsteps approached.

'We need somewhere private where I can kiss you very thoroughly.'

'We've nearly reached my place. It's just around the corner,' Ally replied, ignoring with reckless ease the alarm bells rung by her well-exercised conscience.

They walked quickly. The lift shot up to her apartment, and once inside, Ally switched on the low table lamps. In the warm pool of light, Fletcher looked at her, holding out his arms with a smile that banished any lingering inhibitions. And she walked into them, as eagerly and gladly as if it were what she was born to do. He threaded his fingers through her dark hair.

'You know, Ally, I don't consider myself a wolf. It's not usually my policy to rush these things.'

She felt a ridiculous stab of dismay at the note of caution in his voice.

'Well, to be honest, I like to get to know a man before I let him…kiss me,' she forced herself to admit.

'It's a bit reckless, can be dangerous in fact.'

'It certainly can be,' she muttered, burying her head into his chest and breathing in the mixture of cotton and silk of his clothes combined with the cleanly masculine scent of his skin. Hearing the pounding of his heart.

'So perhaps I should leave now?' he breathed against her cheek, as his fingers gently stroked the nape of her neck.

'Do you really want to know what I think?' she asked, closing her eyes and arching her curves closer into his strength.

'Uh-huh,' he murmured, while his lips trailed dizzying circles over her jaw in a manner that could elicit only one possible answer.

'I think we're wasting valuable time standing here talking.'

CHAPTER TWO

ALLY looked up sleepily as Fletcher emerged from the bathroom, a huge white towel looped around his lean hips. Her breath caught in her throat. All this dark-haired, broad-shouldered, lean-and-muscled masculine perfection was about to walk out of her life just as abruptly as it had appeared. How could the time have flown so quickly?

Monday morning had never felt so bad.

Over the weekend, she and Fletcher had been together for every moment their work commitments spared them, and Ally was delighted to discover that there were so many other wonderful qualities about this man apart from his superb body. She and Fletcher had meshed on so many levels—emotional, physical and intellectual. It had been like meeting a soul mate.

But it had been all too short.

'Did we really only meet two night's ago?' she asked, while her thoughts echoed silently—I feel as if I've known you all my life.

Her knees tucked under her chin, Ally watched from the bed as Fletcher slowly buttoned his shirt, looking down at her with a regretful, thoughtful smile.

He crossed the room to sit on the edge of her mattress. 'I think there's a New Age term for the way we met,' he said. 'We experienced a defining moment.' He lifted his hand as if he were going to reach for her, but stopped, the hand hovering in midair. He sighed and stood up again, reaching instead for the lavender lace nightdress which was crumpled at the bottom of her bed. Tossing it

24

to her, he flashed a cheeky smile. 'And I'd say you've been redefined as a purple passionfruit.'

Ally plucked at the garment. Her fondness for all shades of purple had amused and enchanted Fletcher. Until now it had simply been a colour she often chose to wear because it complemented her dark hair, pale skin and clear, grey eyes. But Fletcher had insisted her favourite colour was symbolic of the newly discovered passionate side to her nature she had never known existed.

She tried desperately to smile back at him. But it was difficult to hide the despair she felt at the reality of Fletcher's leaving. Any minute now the taxi would be pulling up in the street below and he would be walking out of her life, catching the early flight back to North Queensland and his cattle and his outback. He might as well be heading for Mars.

'I suppose you could call our meeting a defining moment,' she said, but then in the next breath, she blurted out, 'But what about the old-fashioned description—love at first sight across a crowded room?'

'Love?' Fletcher looked down at her, startled. 'When I'm about to catch a plane to the back of beyond...' He paused in the act of threading a plaited leather belt through the loops of his jeans and his eyes darkened to a worried navy blue. 'We can't afford to get overly romantic, Ally.'

She felt her face flood with scarlet and a cold hand clamp tightly round her heart. She'd been caught out making the oldest mistake of all. Confusing passionate sex with love and respect and compatibility. Fletcher had never promised her anything more than three nights.

And now their time was up. And she was grown up. This was the real world.

But how could she bear it?

Then it happened just as Ally knew it would. The taxi

arrived, with a screech of tyres and a blast of its horn. Fletcher clasped her to him, kissed her, held her, whispered soothing nothings, kissed her again. And then he was gone. The door closed behind him with a soft sigh and she heard his footsteps on the pavement below, the slam of a car door. And it was all over. Just like that.

She couldn't move. She should have been eating breakfast, dressing for work, but she lay there in the bed wondering how something so wonderful could leave her feeling so lonely and desolate. The usual expectant tingle she felt at the start of the working week had vanished. Her mind, her heart, her body—all of her was numb—a huge gaping vacuum.

Well, she thought with chagrin, Fletcher Hardy had taught her one thing—actually, several if the truth be told. She had never known that lovemaking could be so imaginative, beautiful and exciting all at once. But the end result was her very sure knowledge that she was not the type to enjoy casual sex. It had never happened that way before. Never before had she simply met a man she wanted and thought that alone was an excuse for intimacy. And now she was paying the price for giving away her heart and her body so easily.

She had fallen in love. Hopeless, unreturned love.

She rolled over and buried her head in the pillow, giving in to the luxury of tears—of huge, gasping, noisy sobs.

She wasn't sure how long she had lain there deep in her misery before the phone on her bedside table rang loudly, startling her. Automatically, she lifted the receiver without stopping to consider that she was in no fit state to take a call.

'Hello, Ally. Ally, are you there?'

'Yes,' she blubbered, shoving the bunched-up corner of the sheet into her mouth to stifle more sobs.

'Ally, it's Lucette.'

'Oh, hi. How—how are you?'

'Much better thanks. But I was knocked out by this flu. I can't believe my rotten luck missing the show.'

'Oh, Lucette, you poor thing. I meant to ring you, but—I got caught up. I know that sounds a rather lame excuse. Your set was wonderful! It really was marvellous.'

'I'm glad everything was OK. Do you have the flu now, Ally? You sound awful.'

'My nose is a bit stuffed up,' admitted Ally, reaching for a tissue. 'By the way, I met your cousin,' she added, regretting, even as the words left her lips, her feeble, weak will.

'Fletcher? Really? I hadn't heard from him so I assumed he didn't make it to the show. Poor fellow, I bet he hated it. It's not really his scene at all.'

'Oh, he seemed fairly interested in some aspects of it.'

'What did you think of him?' asked Lucette, a subtle lilt in her voice implying past experience of Fletcher's effect on women. 'Most of my friends think he's pretty cute.'

I'll bet they do, thought Ally with a stab of foolish jealousy. How many other friends of Lucette's had Fletcher dallied with? 'He—he seemed very presentable,' she mumbled.

'Anyhow you'd be wasting your time looking twice at Fletcher,' continued Lucette.

'Oh?' Ally tried for nonchalance, but the word emerged as more of a desperate honk.

'Oh, he has too much bush in his blood. I mean, I grew up in the bush, too—on a property not far from his, but I was glad to leave the outback. But Fletcher will never leave. He's totally committed to his property. Passionate

about the land. So there's not much future for a city girl
with a man like him.'

'Fair enough,' replied Ally, trying to sound bored,
wishing she'd had more common sense than to allow this
conversation to turn to Fletcher. 'Did you read the coverage of our show in the newspapers?' she asked, trying
to steer Lucette back to safer ground.

But she didn't hear Lucette's reply. As she sat there
on her bed, the phone clutched in one hand and a bunch
of tissues in the other, she heard a familiar, authoritative
knock at her front door. Her heart stilled.

Ally dropped the phone, then picked it up and spluttered. 'I—I'm sorry, Lucette. I've got to go.'

Then, her heart thundering in her chest, she bounded
out of bed and snatched up a towelling bathrobe, tying it
around her as she hurried across the room. It couldn't be!
Surely not.

At the front door, she paused and took a deep breath.
Don't be ridiculous, she warned herself. He's on the
plane. This will be someone from work. Get a grip! But
it was a shaking hand she raised to the latch.

She inched the door open. At first, all she could see
was an enormous bunch of Cooktown orchids with lilac
petals and purple throats. But then, from behind them,
came Fletcher's uncertain smile.

'Oh!'

'These were the only purple flowers I could find,' he
said with an apologetic grin and a slight shrug of one
broad shoulder. 'I know it's your favourite colour and—'

'Fletcher, you're still here.'

'I couldn't do it, Ally,' he whispered into her hair as
she flung her arms around him. 'I don't know what this
means, but I couldn't get on that plane. I...'

The rest of his words were lost as she linked her hands
behind his neck and, with a gesture that felt as right and

natural as breathing, pulled his face and his beautiful, sensuous mouth to meet hers.

She managed to wangle a week's special leave. The following days and nights were perfect. They drove into the country and wandered hand in hand through fields of springtime wild flowers. They dined out, cooked for each other, brought home take-away meals and watched movies together. Sensational days and nights. Ally had never had so much fun, had never felt so happy. It was a happiness she knew could not last, but she refused to think about the future, and had absolutely no inclination to think about her work.

And the Cooktown orchids were the first of many purple presents. Fletcher showered her with gifts; chocolate hearts with violet cream centres, a purple velvet evening bag, a box of crystallised violets and finally a beautiful pendant with amethysts set in filigree silver.

Two nights before she was due back at work they lay together on her wide bed, their bodies gleaming in the silvery light of the moon that shone through a high arched window, listening to one of Ally's favourite Brahms sonatas. Rolling onto his side so that, propped on one elbow, he could look into her eyes, Fletcher smiled tenderly. 'I shall never, ever forget you, Ally.' With a long finger, he traced the silvery outline of her body. 'This neat silhouette will be my most precious memory,' he told her, his voice husky.

'I've never been so happy.' She laughed, kissing him. 'I've quite shocked myself.'

Fletcher's blue eyes widened. 'Shocked as in horrified, or shocked as in surprised?'

'Oh, surprised. Very pleasantly surprised.' She bent over him, enjoying the hungry glint in his eyes as her breasts grazed his chest. She nibbled gently at the stubble on his chin. 'I've never been like this before. Wanting to make love over and over. Never having enough.'

'Some people might find that shocking,' Fletcher agreed with a happy chuckle, 'but I don't have a problem with it.'

'So, you're not sleepy yet?' she asked, her voice sultry with desire.

'How could I sleep with your tempting little body draped all over me. Watch out, Ally, you're about to be shocked some more, but I promise you'll love it.' And Fletcher was as good as his word.

The happy bubble burst with a phone call at breakfast.

Ally was making fruit salad, scooping out the fleshy pulp of a passionfruit and laughingly claiming that she bore absolutely no resemblance to the round purple fruit Fletcher had coined as her nickname.

The shrill summons of the telephone came from the lounge room.

'I'll get it,' said Fletcher, helping himself to a cube of mango before he swung his long legs off the pine kitchen stool.

With a contented smile, Ally watched him stride across the room, then she continued to chop banana and squeeze lemon juice over it before adding it to the bowl. She was stirring all the fruits together, delighting in the fresh colour combinations of the different melons—the pale green of honeydew, combined with the deep pink of watermelon and the delicate orange of rockmelon—when she sensed Fletcher standing very still and quiet in the kitchen doorway. She looked up and was startled by his stunned, sad expression.

'Fletcher, what's the matter?'

'There's been an accident,' he said quietly.

Ally felt her stomach lurch with a sudden horrible fear.

She watched him walk towards her slowly, awkwardly, his mouth twisted with the effort to hold his emotions in check. 'My best friend, Jock Lawrence and his wife, Lisa—killed in a car accident in Sydney.'

'Oh, I'm so sorry.'

'Yeah.' Fletcher let out a weary sigh and sank back onto the kitchen stool, his shoulders slumped. Ally quickly moved to the other side of the bench and slipped her arms around him. She rested her cheek gently against his and he turned and kissed her in a brief acknowledgment of her offer of comfort. 'I just can't believe it. He was such a great guy. We went to school, to university…'

There was nothing she could say or do except stay there, holding him, letting him talk slowly, haltingly.

'I'll have to go, Ally. I mean I'd go to the fune-funeral anyway. But there's his son—little Connor. He was the only—only survivor, strapped in one of those little seats in the back. I'm his godfather and, according to old Mr. Lawrence, I've also been named as his guardian.'

'Guardian? Does that mean he'll live with you?'

'Perhaps. I'm not sure yet. He's with his grandparents in Sydney at the moment, but they're pretty old and frail. Jock's father sounded very shaken.' He stood up quickly, so quickly that her hands, as they fell away from his shoulders, slapped against her sides. 'I'll have to ring the airlines and make a booking. Oh, God, I can't believe it.'

Ally followed him into her lounge room and sat some distance away watching as he dialled and waited for a connection, before speaking to the airline. She felt cold and lonely, knowing with a sudden certainty that this time when Fletcher left Melbourne he would be walking out of her life. Going back to his own people—where he belonged.

Eventually he hung up and told her softly. 'I got a cancellation on the 9:00 a.m. flight.'

'This morning?' cried Ally in panic. 'That's only two hours away.'

'I'm sorry, Ally, but Jock's parents—I don't know that they have anyone to help them deal with this.'

'Of course, I understand,' replied Ally, ashamed of her selfish outburst. 'I'll make us a pot of coffee.'

Fletcher was still sitting in the lounge chair, staring thoughtfully at a spot on the rug when she returned. He looked up.

'Smells good.' He smiled, his blue eyes warming as they linked with hers.

She handed him a steaming cup and then sat opposite him, curling her legs beneath her and hugging the mug of coffee to her chest as if for comfort.

'I guess this brings back bad memories for you,' he said gently.

Ally felt her eyebrows lift in surprise. She had told Fletcher just about everything there was to know about her and she guessed that he was referring to her own parents' death in an aeroplane crash when she was seventeen. But that was not on her mind now. Sad as this accident was, all she could think about was what it meant to her relationship with Fletcher. There was so much she wanted to say, had needed to say all week.

In all the talk and all the passion and happiness they shared, they learned a lot about each other, but they skirted round the truth. They had never discussed their future because the horrible truth was that there was no possible future for them. Fletcher's biannual visits to Melbourne were hardly the grounds for an ongoing relationship.

Fletcher put down his cup of coffee and stood up. He looked at her so sadly Ally felt tears spring to her eyes.

'Ally, I'm sorry about this...'

'Don't be, Fletcher. You have to go.'

'No, I mean I'm sorry about us, about coming back and making things worse. If I'd left on Monday...' He reached down and scooped her into his arms. 'I should have been stronger. Should have been able to resist your spell. You're so damn beautiful, Ally.'

How perfectly her body nestled into his. How much she wanted him to go on telling her she was beautiful.

'But what you're trying to say is...we come from two different, totally incompatible worlds,' she said, her voice shaking with the effort to sound calm.

'Too right,' he sighed. 'You do understand, sweetheart, don't you?'

She nodded her head against his chest. Her throat was burning with hot tears. Fletcher's long fingers played with her hair.

'They warn us so much these days about the need for physical protection in a relationship, but that's easy to look after. But protecting our emotions, that's a different story.'

'Perhaps there's a solution,' she couldn't help adding.

'No, I've thought and thought about it. There's no way ahead for us, Ally. You have your career and I have my cattle.'

'City girls have been happy in the country before to-day,' she offered timidly. 'Perhaps I should come and live with you on Wallaroo Downs.'

He broke away from her then, staring at her, his sky blue eyes puzzled, clearly shocked by her words. He shook his head slowly.

'That's a pretty fairy tale, and if it could come true I'd be the happiest man alive, but it wouldn't—it couldn't end in happily ever after.'

Ally felt a painful lump form in her throat, preventing a reply.

'You see,' he continued, the tone in his voice a daunting mixture of tenderness and regret, 'there are more differences between us than my paddocks and your tar and cement. You'd hate the life I lead, Ally. You live in a world you've worked so hard to reach—and it's so elegant and artistic.'

'It's not glamorous all the time,' Ally managed to protest.

'Sewing machine oil is the closest you'd come to grease and dirt,' he said with a lopsided smile that wrenched at her heart. 'I'm just sorry I've messed you up. I've never done anything so damned stupid in my life before.'

Ally's chin came up defiantly. 'I don't think it was at all stupid. I've never had anything so wonderful happen to me—ever.'

Fletcher groaned and pulled her to him. 'Listen, passionfruit,' he whispered, 'I have to pack and then I'm going to Sydney. And after that I'll almost certainly have to get back to Wallaroo. There's a muster coming up and I have to be back for that. Then, with a bit of luck, there'll be a wet season. I can't see us getting together again in a long while. You're a beautiful, clever woman and this is where you belong. You have to get on with your brilliant career. There's no other way of looking at this.'

She knew that as a woman of the nineties she should be able to handle this. People had relationships and then they moved on. It was as simple as that. It happened all around her all the time.

But not to her.

Ally glanced at the clock on the wall behind Fletcher.

If he were to make it to his flight, he would have to get moving.

'I'll check out the laundry basket. See if you've left anything there,' she said grimly with a small, dismissive shrug of her shoulders.

Fletcher packed in silence while Ally tidied the kitchen. They had never been so quick and efficient together. She insisted on driving him to the airport.

As her small sedan zipped along the freeway, she tried to forget about her own sadness and think of the poor little boy left without parents.

'This little boy, Connor. Do you know him very well?' she asked.

'No. I have to admit, I haven't seen all that much of him,' admitted Fletcher. 'I went to his christening when he was just a tiny tadpole—hadn't even reached the ankle-biter stage. He must be three or four now. Last time I saw him he'd just started toddling around. As far as I remember, he looks like Jock.' His voice broke a little. 'Brown hair and eyes—going to be tall.'

Once they reached the busy, bustling airport, and Fletcher had queued then checked in, there was little time for conversation. And there was certainly no privacy for the kinds of things Ally would have liked to discuss. All too soon the flight to Sydney was boarding and for the last time she felt Fletcher's strong arms around her, and his warm, delicious lips on hers.

'Be beautiful, Ally,' he whispered, his eyes glistening with a betraying dampness. Then he swung away quickly and strode through the doors of the departure lounge, leaving her without looking back.

She was prepared for his silence; she hadn't expected him to ring her from Sydney. And she was prepared for the sense of desolation that swamped her. But what she hadn't expected was the lassitude with which she returned to her work. She'd hoped that once back in the swing of things, the old enthusiasm for dealing with designs, textiles and market trends and the fascinating array of individuals associated with that world would rescue her from her misery.

It was with a growing sense of alarm that she faced each day at the office. She took her designs home to work on at night, hoping the soothing atmosphere of her own apartment would help inspiration to flow. With the spring and summer collection behind her, Ally had to plan for next year's winter season and a juicy contract with the wool board was on offer. Normally she would have been thrilled. But she couldn't concentrate and what was worse, much, much worse, she couldn't bring herself to care.

Her mind and her emotions were totally absorbed with Fletcher. Where was he now? Had he gone back to North Queensland? Had he taken little Connor with him? Did he think about her the way she thought endlessly of him?

After three weeks of silence and despair, she could stand it no longer. She had to make some kind of contact with him. Her first step was to ring Lucette.

'Have I heard from Fletcher, Ally?' Lucette repeated, her voice squeaking with surprise at Ally's first question once the greetings were over. 'Why, yes, I have actually. He rang from North Queensland just yesterday.'

'You see,' Ally offered with a silly little laugh, 'I ended up seeing quite a bit of him while he was down here, but then he was called away for the funeral...' Her voice trailed away as her tightly strung nerves clenched a notch tighter.

The stunned silence on the other end of the line didn't help her feel any more relaxed.

'Really?' Lucette managed at last.

'Does he have the little boy with him?'

'No, not yet. Connor's still in Sydney with his grand-parents. But as a matter of fact that's why Fletcher rang me. He's guardian for Connor and he wants me to find a nanny to travel up to Wallaroo Downs and help take care of him there.'

Ally closed her eyes against the frightening wave of dizziness that swamped her as a host of different pictures crowded her mind: pictures of Fletcher, sun-tanned, astride a horse somewhere in North Queensland; of Fletcher and a little brown-haired, brown-eyed boy walk-ing hand in hand along a shady creek bank; of a young attractive nanny living with them both day in, day out.

'Ally, are you still there?'

'Yes, Lucette. I'm here. Listen, would you mind ter-ribly much if I came and visited you? I need to talk.'

'That's fine,' replied Lucette, unable to disguise her surprise. 'I'll be home all evening. You have my ad-dress?'

'But, Ally, this is impossible!' Lucette exclaimed an hour later as the two women sat opposite each other at the kitchen table in her tiny bed-sit apartment. 'For starters you underestimate the stubbornness of the Hardy male. There's no way Fletcher would have someone like you as a nanny on Wallaroo Downs.'

Ally's chest tightened painfully at Lucette's words.

'I think Fletcher came to care for me. In fact I know he did.'

Something in her expression seemed to capture Lucette's attention. She stared at Ally for several silent moments and then she reached over and took Ally's hand.

'I'm sure he does feel very strongly about you,' she said gently. 'Fletcher's usually very wary about getting entangled with women, because of where he lives. He believes only women who grow up in the bush can take the harsh life of the outback. So if he allowed you to understand he cared...' Lucette paused and smiled rue-fully. 'Then I'd say chances are he was totally smitten.'

'I'm prepared to take a gamble on it.'

'But your career!' Lucette cried. 'How could you pos-sibly turn your back on everything you've achieved?'

'I don't know,' admitted Ally. 'A month ago I would have said it was totally impossible, but...' She paused, taking in a deep shuddering breath. 'Have you ever been in love, Lucette?'

'Of course,' the girl laughed, 'hundreds of times.'

'No. I'm talking the real thing. I can't go on without him. I can't work. I can't eat or sleep.' She paused and shook her head at Lucette's wide-eyed response. 'I can't believe I'm saying all this. I used to be the first person to condemn girls who went all drippy over males. I mean, I used to think that all it took to resist falling into that kind of trap was a modicum of intelligence. But honestly, Lucette, I've no choice. I've got to go to him.'

Lucette sighed and refilled Ally's coffee cup. 'Ally, I really feel for you, believe me. But I don't think Fletcher would have a bar of it. And it wouldn't be because he doesn't care for you. It's simply that he couldn't imag-ine how you could possibly be happy out there. He'd worry about taking you away from everything you've achieved.' Lucette eyed her crestfallen friend with con-cern. 'This is all my fault!'

'What do you mean?'

'Well, if I hadn't been so jolly eager to show off my set designs when he was in Melbourne for that confer-ence, he would never have come to the show and fallen for the lovely Alexandra Fraser.'

Ally closed her stinging, tear-filled eyes as she remem-bered that moment when a tall, dark grazier marched into the models' dressing room! She stared into her coffee cup. 'I think I've got to do it, Lucette. I'm prepared for everyone telling me I'm mad. I'm prepared for Fletcher to be a little angry at first, but I think he'll get over it. It's just that I've found someone I love more than my career and I think I can convince him of that, too. I've fallen in love and I can't just sit here and do absolutely zilch about it!'

'Well, apart from anything else we've covered, there might still be one major hitch,' said Lucette tentatively.

'Which is?' asked Ally, lifting her chin in a brave effort at defiance.

'What experience have you had as a nanny?'

'Aha! I can answer that,' cried Ally triumphantly. 'All the time I was at college, I worked as a nanny for the Johnstons. You know Dr. James Johnston and his wife Helen—the paediatricians? Nights, weekends, holidays. I looked after their four children on and off for three and a half years.'

Lucette raised her fair eyebrows and looked back at Ally with eyes the same sky blue as Fletcher's. She took a long, deep swig of her coffee. 'Then perhaps we'd better take a closer look at this,' she said with a solemnity which was totally spoiled when her face broke into a cheeky grin, again alarmingly like her cousin's. 'But we're going to have to plan it all very carefully.'

CHAPTER THREE

THE best laid plans of mice and men... The unwelcome quotation flashed through Ally's mind again as it had on repeated occasions over recent weeks. But now, with Connor's little hand clinging to hers as she crossed the steamy car park at Townsville airport, she refused to think of defeat. Together with Lucette, she had schemed and plotted so that this risky enterprise would run like clockwork and the journey was almost complete.

She'd been nervous about going to Sydney to meet Connor, but the few days she'd spent there getting to know the little boy had been delightful. They had enjoyed a trip to the beach and to Taronga Park Zoo, as well as some quiet times at his grandparents' house. Then, to her relief, he had come with her and Lucette on the plane flight to Townsville without objection. All that was left was the final leg—driving out to Wallaroo Downs.

And to Fletcher.

Ally shifted the weight of her large carry bag higher onto her shoulder and smiled at Connor, who looked back at her with trusting, big brown eyes.

'This should be our vehicle,' said Lucette, indicating a sturdy-looking station wagon in the line-up of hire cars. She pushed their heavily loaded luggage carrier the last few metres and clicked the central locking button on her key. 'Hey, presto! Look, Connor,' Lucette cried as she swung the car door open. 'Magic doors!'

But Ally could feel Connor backing away, his hand in hers struggling to be freed.

'No!' he cried. 'No! I don't like that car!' His little face contorted in fear as he tried to pull away.

Ally dropped to her knees and threw her arms around him.

'No!' he sobbed. 'I don't like that car!' His voice rose in alarm, but he clung to Ally. She could feel his little body trembling and her heart nearly broke for him.

'Oh, you poor darling,' Ally murmured as she hugged him to her. She realised at once that his parents must have been driving a similar car when they were taken from him so horrifically.

Lucette hovered uncertainly near the luggage.

'Sweetheart, look. I've got something to show you,' Ally said as she dipped her hand into the large carry bag and drew out a soft toy she'd been keeping for such a moment.

The sobs subsided slightly. 'What—what is it?' Connor hiccupped, staring through his tears at the furry brown creature Ally held.

'It's a platypus, Connor. I had him made just for you.' A plump little hand reached tentatively towards the ball of fur.

'Plat-pus?' he whispered.

'That's right,' said Ally. 'See, he has a fluffy tummy and a lovely black bill and four little black feet.'

Connor fingered one webbed foot, beautifully crafted from the finest black leather.

'That's amazing,' exclaimed Lucette from behind them. 'It's so lifelike. Did you have it made at work?'

Ally nodded. 'A few people owed me favours.' She spoke to Connor. 'Real platypuses live in creeks out in the bush. And that's where we're going. Uncle Fletcher lives there, too.'

'Can I hold the plat-pus?'

'Of course you can, darling. He's yours to keep.'

Aware that Lucette was quietly loading their luggage into the back of the station wagon, Ally continued talking as Connor cuddled his new toy. 'When I was a little girl, my favourite story was about a platypus called Shy. Would you like me to tell it to you?'

The little boy nodded solemnly, blinking away his tears.

'Well let's you, me and your platypus make ourselves comfortable in the back of the car here and I'll tell you about Shy.' Ally held her breath as she gently guided Connor towards the car door. He hesitated and turned to her.

'Can I call my plat-pus Shy?'

'Of course you can. It's a lovely name, isn't it,' Ally reassured him, and he allowed himself to be buckled into his car seat without another murmur.

And as Ally began her story of the platypus family who lived in the riverbank, Lucette slipped into the driver's seat and the car slowly edged out into the traffic.

Shy had been a big hit with Connor, Ally reflected hours later, as she sedately guided a gentle mare down a quiet bush track at Wallaroo Downs. One hurdle had been cleared, but a still higher one faced her. She had yet to discover how Fletcher would react when he returned from a day's branding to find her already settled into his home.

Grateful for the shady protection of whispering casuarinas, she tried to shrug off her nervousness by focusing on the soothing sounds of the quiet bush; the steady clip, clop of Juno's careful steps and the peaceful hum of cicadas in the trees around her.

No wonder Fletcher loved his outback. It was so remote, so alien in its stark, dry beauty—another world. Separated from Melbourne by thousands of kilometres, it was hard to believe she was still in the same country. On the drive inland from Townsville airport they'd travelled through heat and dust and past endless paddocks of brown, lifeless-looking stubble, but here, by the creek, it was cool and shady and perfectly serene.

Until…the afternoon peace was split by the sudden roar of a motorbike.

To Ally's horror, her startled horse whinnied and reared, hooves striking at the air. Then, within breathless seconds, she felt the reins snatched from her trembling hands and a furious voice roared at her.

'Alexandra? What the hell are you doing here?'

Panic flared!

Common sense should have told her the danger was over. The dreadful motorbike's engine had cut off, the mare was calming down and the bush was quickly returning to its former languid stillness. So she knew the wild thumping of her heart was an overreaction. There was no longer any excuse for her to crouch low against Juno's neck with her eyes squeezed tightly shut.

Except that she knew that voice.

She knew exactly who was bellowing at her and it was the very last person she wanted to meet until all her plans were in place.

He wasn't supposed to be down here!

With trepidation, she lifted her head, blinked, and her stomach clenched. A fiercely scowling Fletcher stood within arm's reach, Juno's reins gripped tightly in one strong brown hand.

She found herself fighting a nervous urge to look away, yet she forced her eyes to hold Fletcher's scalding gaze. Agitated as she was, she couldn't stifle a swift glow of admiration. He was as rugged and tall, as wide-shouldered and lean-limbed as the memory she had treasured these past weeks. And his eyes, piercing blue as ever, were a perfect match for the flashes of brilliant sky she glimpsed between the swamp bloodwoods behind him. But the smile, the special, heart-flipping grin, was missing. She had never known Fletcher not to smile at her!

This was nothing like the reception she had hoped for and pictured hundreds of times during the last few weeks. She manoeuvred her strained features into something resembling a smile.

'Er...hello, Fletcher... I'm, um, I'm practising riding.'

'I see.' His clipped reply dropped unhelpfully into the space between them.

Ally shivered. It was then she noticed the trail bike he'd abandoned when she and Juno blundered onto his path, now slewed against an old tree stump a metre or so behind him. The realisation of her guilt sent her heart sinking further.

'I'm sorry I nearly ran into you.'

The apology was clearly not accepted. Fletcher merely continued to glare at her in silent anger while her wretched eyes took in more details. His crow-black hair, his bare chest and shoulders all glistened with water and his jeans clung to his hips and thighs in dark, damp patches that blatantly outlined his flagrant masculinity.

'You've been swimming?' she stammered.

'Yes,' he replied. The briefest flicker of a smile twitched the corners of his mouth. 'If you'd been a few minutes earlier, you would have found me in the creek.'

Heat stole into her cheeks. He would have been swimming naked. She had no doubt about that.

She whipped her eyes away from his damp lower region as he growled at her, without smiling. 'I suppose it's too much to ask for an explanation as to why you've suddenly appeared here, and just happen to be riding one of my horses without any invitation?'

'I was planning to give you a very good explanation.'

'Planning, Ally? Hell! You practically caused a serious accident.'

His hostility was enough to wither her tiny stock of courage even before she began to defend herself.

'I said I'm sorry.' Ally's grey eyes blazed briefly, then her lashes lowered over them as she mumbled her excuse. 'Your stockman said I could use this horse—that you were out branding somewhere. I didn't know—'

'You came over three thousand kilometres just to take in a little horse riding practice?'

She nearly lost her nerve there and then. Clearly he regarded her as an intruder—uninvited and unwanted. Tears gathered swiftly, burning the backs of her lids.

How could this happen? This was the man she loved! This was her Fletcher! He had come to the city and made exquisite love to her and changed her life forever. But now he had the audacity to glare at her with outright rejection clearly stamped in the firm set of his jaw, the frowning black stripe of his eyebrows and the white-knuckled clench of his fists.

She took an agonising breath hoping to calm her frantic, self-defeating thoughts. 'You're surprised to see me,' she whispered, and her wide eyes anxiously darted away from his unyielding gaze.

'Surprise is one word I could choose, I guess,' Fletcher drawled, his deep voice rumbling with sarcasm. But now he was staring back at her, hard. His eyes travelled— very deliberately—over her slim frame, her jeans and soft, white shirt buttoned low over a pale lavender crop top. They rested for the longest time on her pale face. 'What are you doing here?' he repeated, his voice less harsh this time, as if he had run out of breath suddenly.

'I—I've— Your cousin and I have brought your little godson—Connor.' The words tumbled out of control like beads spilling from a broken necklace.

Fletcher scowled. 'You came with Lucette?'

'Yes. You're his guardian now...'

'I know damn well I'm his guardian, but what I still don't understand is what you've got to do with it?'

'Well, Lucette was looking for a nanny for Connor so that you...'

'You're sidetracking,' Fletcher snapped. 'Get to the point.'

'Well, the point is,' resumed Ally, running her tongue nervously over parched lips. 'I'm his nanny.'

'What?'

Startled, Ally watched as the colour in Fletcher's face deepened and then leached away while, with the worst sense of timing, a kookaburra broke into raucous laughter in a gum tree overhanging the track.

'Hell, Ally! You can't be!'

'I've had some training as a nanny,' she offered tentatively, then began to chew the inside of her cheek while her fingers nervously played with the horse's mane.

'Damn it to hell! Of all the crazy...!' He studied her through narrowed eyes. 'How much?'

'How much what?' she repeated lamely.

'How much training have you done to be a nanny for heaven's sake?'

'That's how I put myself through Art College—working as a nanny for...'

Interrupting her with a fierce curse, Fletcher tossed the reins back over Juno's neck before striding across the track away from her, shaking his head, clearly unimpressed, quite obviously more angry than ever.

'I know it might look as if I'm trying to profit from a little boy's tragedy,' Ally called after him.

But he ignored her.

Snatching a faded blue cotton shirt from the seat of his trail bike, he shrugged his broad brown back into it and

Ally half expected to see the thin cotton split beneath the savagery of his movements. He prowled slowly back to her and when he spoke again, his voice was weary—as if he had fought a long battle.

'You've spent years of training and hard work to become a leading bloody fashion designer, so stop spinning me this yarn about nannies and tell me what you're really doing here, Alexandra Fraser?'

Ally gulped. This was all so dreadfully different from how their meeting was meant to be. She could see her careful plans collapsing as helplessly as a child's sandcastle beneath the tide. Of course, she had expected Fletcher to be surprised, even shocked when she arrived on his property out of the blue, but she had never dreamed that their meeting would be so...so vitriolic.

This was certainly not the time to confess that she had given up everything just to be here with him. She felt another blush mount embarrassingly into her cheeks as she mentally dumped her real reason, that she wanted to spend the rest of her life at his side. If he had caught her red-handed, duffing his precious cattle, he couldn't have scowled at her with any more venom.

But, she acknowledged wretchedly, she'd come a long way and, while now, face-to-face with Fletcher and his outback, nothing seemed clear and logical like it had in Melbourne, she really had no choice but to hang on to her pride and continue. She straightened her shoulders.

'I have told you,' she began frostily. 'I want to stay here and be Connor's nanny. As you know I lost my own parents in a plane crash when I was seventeen.... I was much older than Connor, of course, but I do understand something of what he's going through.... Besides,' she offered a tiny white lie, 'Lucette had all sorts of trouble trying to find someone suitable.'

'Someone suitable?' He laughed bitterly and the blue

eyes glittered coldly. 'I thought Lucette would have known better. She grew up on a cattle property and knows what it's like here. She couldn't have found anyone less suitable than you.'

'No-o!'

He might just as well have slapped her hard. As if in sympathy, the mare stepped sideways with a swaying lurch. Ally reached for the pommel to steady herself and if possible, her cheeks burned even hotter.

Surely she was the biggest love-struck fool in all history! Somehow she forced herself to stare back at Fletcher's glowering face, but as she did so, Ally was compelled to ask herself the dreadful, but oh so obvious question—how in heaven's name had she ever been so certain that this man loved her?

'Let's go back to the homestead to sort this out.' Fletcher's businesslike voice broke into her wretched thoughts. 'I take it you didn't just dump my godson on the doorstep. Lucette stayed behind with Connor?'

'Yes,' Ally managed, blinking back tears. 'But she can't stay for long. She's going on to Richmond this evening.'

'And then she'll leave you holding the baby?'

'But I don't mind at all. And he's hardly a baby. He's four and he's an absolute darling—a bright, good little boy.'

'Of course he is. Jock, his dad, was the finest mate a man could ever want. But for Pete's sake, Ally, you could have warned me that he was coming...' Fletcher paused and Ally looked away guiltily, unable to meet his accusatory gaze.

'I should apologise,' she said softly. 'The secrecy was deliberate—a kind of surprise.' It seemed absurd now, but she had hoped the element of surprise would give her an advantage. In her career, she'd always had to plan ahead, anticipating breaks, then snatching opportunities whenever they presented themselves. And she certainly hadn't wanted to allow Fletcher the opportunity to reject her out of hand before she at least had the chance to see him again.

But clearly seeing him had been no help at all.

'It shouldn't be too hard to get a quick replacement nanny,' he said grimly. She opened her mouth to try to reply, but this time could find no words at all.

How could Fletcher be so unfeeling when they had been so close? Close? she thought ruefully. They had been inseparable! Now, he could at the very least be kind; he must have realised that she wouldn't have come so far unless she cared for him very much. Tears stung her eyes and she blinked them away quickly.

'Move back behind the saddle,' he commanded, his tone underlined by a new note of challenge.

Shock waves jolted through Ally so that her voice emerged as a pitiful squeak.

'You're getting onto my horse?'

'My horse,' he reminded her with scalding accuracy.

How could she possibly have him so alarmingly close when her nerves were already stretched unbearably? Surely her heart rate would go through the roof! Her anxiety must have amused him, for the faintest glimmer of a smile dusted his features.

'What about your motorbike?' she asked, her voice faltering.

'It'll be quite safe here for now. Now make room.' He fitted a boot to the stirrup. 'You look like you're going to fall off Juno any minute.' With his face now only inches from hers, her heart beat a frantic tattoo. Up close, his mouth, even when it was grim and disapproving, was gorgeous—surely designed for passion rather than barking orders?

'Get back,' he muttered abruptly, and indicated with a jerk of his head that she should move quickly. Ally scrambled to obey and Fletcher swung a long leg over Juno's back and slid into the saddle. 'Hang on!'

His order was accompanied by a flick of the reins and Juno took off at a brisk canter. Ally's arms instinctively flew around him and as she clung to his hard, muscled back, the electricity of the contact nearly stopped her heart altogether. But any thrill soon short-circuited as Fletcher yelled over his shoulder, his voice just reaching her over Juno's pounding hooves, 'This is a bloody mess, Ally. You know I told you not to come out here.'

'Don't say it!' Ally pleaded with Lucette hours later as they sat on the wide front veranda of the magnificent Wallaroo Downs homestead. 'I underestimated the stubbornness of the Hardy male.'

They had finally settled a rather puzzled Connor to sleep in the strange, old-fashioned, brass and iron bed with its voluminous mosquito net. Fletcher was closeted in his study at the end of the hall, presumably attacking some important paperwork.

'Even I was shocked at just how keen he was to get rid of you,' commented Lucette.

Ally's chest tightened painfully at the accuracy of her friend's words. Fletcher had insisted that she leave as soon as possible. 'You tried to warn me,' she sighed. 'I thought you made up all that stuff about the kind of woman needed in the bush. But Fletcher believes it!'

'He also believes,' added Lucette, 'something he read once about fashion design being your passion, fulfilling you totally...'

'Well...' responded Ally, 'people change. I've...metamorphosed.'

She thumped the flat wooden arm of the squatter's

chair with a force that made her wince, as she slumped in its comfortable canvas seat, her mind full of choking unhappiness. Then she rallied, her anger surfacing again. 'What right has Fletcher to suggest that I'm likely to leave a job half-done just because I get sick of the scenery?'

'If anyone can stick at something in spite of difficulties, it's you, Ally,' Lucette agreed as she dumped her overnight bag at the top of the veranda steps, ready for her departure. Part of their 'perfect' scheme had included Lucette's leaving as soon as possible after she had escorted Ally and Connor onto the property.

Ally stared out into the black night beyond the glow cast by the homestead lights. The two friends sat in miserable silence.

'I'd better go.' Lucette's voice interrupted Ally's misery. 'It's a good four hours to Richmond and Mum and Dad will worry.'

At Lucette's words, Ally realised that this was her chance to acknowledge her mistake and get out before this ridiculous venture turned into a full-scale disaster. She could go with Lucette to their property at Richmond, and from there she could catch a bus to the coast. She could be back in Melbourne in a day or two.

'I guess I may as well leave now, too. Fletcher will soon find another woman to look after Connor. And he and Mrs. Harrison can cope between them in the meantime,' she said with an exhausted sigh.

'No,' came a deep voice from the darkness of the unlit hallway behind them. 'That's not convenient.'

Fletcher stepped onto the veranda. Ally's heart stilled and she attempted a smile, but the evening's argument repeated on her. Her face felt painfully stiff from holding back unshed tears of disappointment.

'I certainly will find a suitable nanny as soon as possible, but as you have arrived without warning, Ally, I will need your help tomorrow. Ned tells me stock are getting out of the five mile paddock. We've got to mend the fence there in the morning. And Mary Harrison will shortly have her hands full feeding the mustering crew. She won't have time to keep an eye on a youngster, as well.'

'That's fine,' answered Ally in a flat monotone, but contradicting the voice, her spirits lifted ridiculously at the knowledge that she was needed on Wallaroo Downs, at least for a short time. She was smiling as Lucette's Land Cruiser took off into the dark night.

Ally watched the twin red eyes of the vehicle's rear lights winking as the car wound its way along the bush track. She was excruciatingly aware that, apart from the old stockman and his wife, and a few stable hands and ringers, who had retired to their own cottages for the night, she was now alone, kilometres from anywhere, with Fletcher.

He stood beside her on the veranda, also watching the retreating vehicle, his hand resting near hers on the timber railing. She stole a quick glimpse at his profile as he continued staring into the inky depths of the bush. For a moment she had to shut her eyes. What was it about this man that so totally wrecked her equilibrium?

But she knew the answer. His rugged masculinity and natural earthiness tugged savagely at her senses. She carefully glanced his way again. There seemed to be nothing to talk about now that their favourite topic—how they felt about each other—was taboo.

'We just might be lucky and get some rain.'

His words brought a weak smile to her lips. She should have guessed he would choose something innocuous like the weather.

'How can you tell?' Ally asked, trying to make her

voice sound calm. He smelled delicious and she was
swamped by memories of his arms around her, the heat
of his hard body meshed with hers and the heady taste
of his lips.

Sensations she would never experience again.

She forced herself to follow his gaze up into the sky,
looking for indications of rain. And she wondered
vaguely where the moon was. The world beyond the veranda was pitch black, but then that was to be expected
at night, wasn't it?

'No stars,' he said. 'Out here, away from city lights,
we usually have hundreds, thousands of stars. They're all
covered by cloud, now. It doesn't always mean rain, but
you never know. There's a low up in the Gulf.'

'I guess you need rain badly.'

'That's a bit of an understatement,' he said harshly. 'It
hasn't rained here for three years.'

'Of course, I did know about the drought.' She tried
to cover for herself quickly. Hadn't she driven through
endless kilometres of dusty, drought-stricken country?

'Drought, floods, bushfires. It all happens here,' he
said. 'It's not an easy life.'

'I never thought it was,' whispered Ally, looking away,
her heart thumping wildly as she realised how quickly
their conversation had come dangerously close to the
heart of their disagreement—the question of her suitabil-
ity to life in the bush.

The same thought must have occurred to Fletcher because he thrust his hands deep in the pockets of his jeans
and quickly steered the conversation back to safer
ground.

'Of course, it probably won't rain. The weather fore-
casters have said it will and they never get it right.' He
laughed raggedly. 'If we really are going to get a wet
this year, the rivers will come up and cut us off. It could

happen anytime from now on. So we'll have to get you out of here, soon.'

Ally felt her lower lip droop forward. With a supreme effort of will she drew it in, sucking in a deep breath at the same time. She had to try again, to really get to the bottom of the reason he wanted her to go.

In spite of all the words that had been flung back and forth earlier in the evening, she could not bring herself to believe that Fletcher didn't feel the same need for her now as he had in Melbourne. There was a tension, a guarded wariness about him, that signalled to her he was afraid of releasing telltale emotions. To become a good designer she'd also had to be a sensitive artist. She'd learned to look beneath people's exteriors, to really study them, watching their reactions, learning to read their real moods. It seemed to Ally that Fletcher was displaying an awful lot of tension just to tell her she was unsuitable for the job.

'You think if I lived here, I'd let you down, don't you?' she began.

If it was possible he stiffened even further at her words.

'You would soon get sick of it.'

'Not—' She was glad that he was still facing away from her, his profile in deep shadow. At least she couldn't see his reaction as the pride she had so tenaciously clung to fell into tatters. 'Not with you here. I'd never tire of you, Fletcher.'

Fletcher's blue eyes seared into Ally's upturned, pleading face.

'You don't think it could happen, but you would soon grow tired of the life out here, hundreds of miles from anywhere. No city, no friends, no fashion except jeans and riding boots.'

'I hear they have some pretty glamorous outback balls,' Ally said with an effort to smile.

But ignoring her comment, he stepped towards her, his face dark and intense. 'There's no way I would take you away from your career. I know how much you love it. I understand what you've sacrificed to get to the top.'

From somewhere deep inside, Ally dredged a final morsel of courage. 'But,' she began, as confidently as she could, 'you haven't taken me away. I've left of my own accord. I was happy to resign.'

'What?' Fletcher looked as if he had been slugged by an unexpected sniper's bullet. There was a visible slump in his broad shoulders and his mouth hung open. 'You're mad,' he whispered. 'Resigned? This is insanity!'

'You see,' Ally whispered back, her voice trembling along with her entire body. 'I want you more than all that, Fletcher.'

He thumped his fist onto the veranda railing with such force she was sure he must have hurt himself. Then he stared once more out into the night and his voice when he spoke again was gravelly, as if he had swallowed stones.

'No, Ally. I won't let you give it all up. You're too damned good. I sat in the audience in that show down south and saw all those people watching you, cheering you, saw the journalists flocking round you. They love you. They'd never forgive me for taking you away.'

Her vision was suddenly blurry.

'Poor Fletcher,' she whispered. 'How can I make you understand? They would let me go if they knew how happy I was.'

Ally reached out shaking fingers and lightly touched Fletcher's hand as he continued to grasp the veranda railing. Holding her breath, she traced with her forefinger the veins standing out against the sun-tanned skin. Her own body was so tight with tension that Fletcher's trembling response to her fingertips startled her.

Slowly, agonisingly slowly, he turned her small white hand over in his and then lifted it to his cheek and Ally's breath caught in her throat when the familiar, masculine roughness of his day-old beard grazed her palm.

I've lost all my self-respect, she thought dazedly, as, standing on tiptoe, she ran the tip of her pink tongue over her lips, then licked at his earlobe. 'Fletcher, aren't you even a little bit glad to see me?' she whispered.

He didn't flinch, but out of the corner of her eye, Ally glimpsed a muscle twitch in his cheek, twice, and then his eyes fixed on the curve of her mouth. She stifled a sob as she watched a brief but unmistakable tremor pass across his strong features.

'Oh, for heaven's sake, Ally,' he murmured huskily, and released her hand only to reach out and almost, but not quite, touch her dusky pink cheek.

They stood in awkward silence, his lean, brown hand hovering inches away from her and his blue eyes glittering while he stared at her in the soft moonlight. Nervously she returned his gaze as he lingered over each separate detail. Holding her breath, she watched as he allowed his eyes to travel slowly over the silky, dark frame of her hair and the outline of her face. His gaze rested on her eyes as if he were committing their colour and texture to memory. Finally he focused, as if mesmerised, on her lips, and she could sense just how ripe and rosy they were, ready for kissing. His breath expelled wearily on a long sigh. With a groan, Fletcher dipped his hands into the silky dark tresses of her hair and drew her to him.

How wonderful he smelled. She buried her face into the soft cotton of his shirt, relishing the warm, musky strength of the chest beneath and allowing the comforting tenderness of his embrace to seep into her. This was where she belonged. He could protest all he liked about their incompatibility, but with Fletcher's strong arms holding her close, she knew differently.

Her ears caught the erratic racing of his heartbeat and she looked up in alarm, only to meet his mouth reaching for hers. Hungrily, desperately, his lips drank at hers and his arms crushed her to him. He tasted divine. His invasion of her mouth was so intimate, so right! This mouth, these hands, this lean, powerful body linked to hers felt so perfect it was almost frightening. She began to shake.

'Ally,' he groaned, his voice raspy with longing. 'I want you so much.'

'Well, my darling,' she stammered, 'I—I'm here and—and I'm yours.'

Then she was winding her arms around his neck and threading her urgent fingers into the rough curls that lay against his collar. She clung to him, moulding her slender curves temptingly against the solid muscles of his chest and thighs, knowing full well she was exploiting his weakness.

'No!'

The single syllable had never sounded so terrible. As it tore from Fletcher's lips, he wrenched himself away with a force that spun Ally against the veranda rail. He stood some distance away, staring at her, his breathing ragged. 'I made enough mistakes in Melbourne,' he gasped. 'This has got to stop, Ally.'

Why? she wanted to cry. Why, when it was so obvious that they belonged in each other's embrace as surely as birds belonged to the skies? But she couldn't bear to hear all over again his litany of reasons for rejecting her. Although she remained silent, her body protested loudly.

Her hands fluttered in frustrated gestures of helplessness and she shook her head desperately.

Gently, his hands, reaching to cup either side of her face, stilled the motion, and with his thumbs, Fletcher wiped the tears on her cheeks. 'It's time to face reality, Ally. There's no future for us, so we shouldn't even begin to pretend that there is.' Then he stepped away, gesturing along the veranda. 'Now let me show you to your room.'

Sleepless hours later, a dreadful noise erupted above Ally. It was still pitch-black as she sat up in bed, startled by a roaring clamour pelting on the corrugated iron roof above where she'd been trying to sleep.

'Rain!' she heard Fletcher shout from the veranda outside her door.

Leaping from her bed, Ally ran to her doorway.

'Doesn't it smell wonderful? Don't you just love that sound?' Fletcher called to her.

Ally's nose twitched as her nostrils caught the musty, metallic odour of dampening earth. Fletcher was dancing wildly along the veranda. His powerful naked body gleamed in the flashes of white lightning and, as if to match the wild elements outside, a ripple of uncontrollable, useless longing like a roll of thunder, ignited low within her.

But before she could submit to more self-pity, a little wail reached her ears through the roar of the driving rain.

Connor! Of course! He would be terrified by the racketing noise. She swung back into her room to gather up the clothes she'd left beside her bed and dragged them on quickly, as the poor little boy's cries grew more frightened.

'Can't you hear him?' she called at Fletcher as she charged past him, along the veranda to Connor's room.

'What's that?' he cried, obviously deafened by rain and the excited barking of the station dogs.

'Put some clothes on,' she yelled back.

Connor was such a tiny, trembling heap, lost in the big bed, that she could only just see him even when she switched on the lamp. She quickly gathered him to her.

'Hush, sweetheart,' she murmured into his warm cheek. 'It's okay. I'm here now. You know it's only rain.'

'Rain?' Connor looked up at her with huge, disbelieving brown eyes. She could guess what he was thinking. How could this dreadful hammering be rain? Rain in the city never sounded like this.

'I thought it was the accident,' he whispered, and buried his head against her chest and began to sob. Ally held him tight and rocked him back and forth.

'No, no, no,' she crooned, remembering how the nightmares had continued for many months after her own parents' accident. 'It's all right. It's all right. You're safe.'

A shadow fell across them. She looked up. Fletcher was beside her, dressed in jeans but bare-chested. 'He's frightened,' she said quietly. 'He remembers the car crash of course.' Even though she spoke softly, Connor heard her and his sobs broke out afresh. 'Hush, baby, hush,' she whispered. 'Perhaps some warm milk?' she asked Fletcher, and he was gone in an instant.

When he returned, it was to find Connor much calmer, still curled in Ally's arms. She took the china mug of milk from him.

'I put some honey in it, too,' he said.

'Wonderful, thanks.' Ally smiled at him and thought how gorgeous he looked with his hair all tousled and dark stubble lining his jaw. 'I'll stay the rest of the night with him.'

He reached down and stroked the little boy's soft damp curls, his blue eyes dark and brooding. 'Thanks for looking after him. His dad was a special guy. I really want him to be happy here.' Then he squeezed Ally's shoulder and with a regretful smile, he turned to leave. 'Catch you later,' he whispered, and she smiled back, silent but unaccountably happy.

Then she settled down beside Connor and cuddled the warm, sleepy child gently in her arms. Perhaps things would turn out all right, after all, she thought with a contented sigh. If she just had enough time to show Fletcher that she could fit into the outback way of life, perhaps he would change his mind. Perhaps he would admit that he really did love her.

Perhaps they could have a future.

It seemed only minutes later that she heard a footstep on the floorboards nearby. She forced leaden eyes open to see Fletcher standing over her. Her first reaction was to smile, but in the dim, grey light she watched the initial softness in his eyes vanish and the hardening of his jaw told her something was wrong.

The rain was falling as forcefully as ever.

'What time is it?'

'Half past eight. You've been asleep for hours. Listen. The river's rising already. We're going to have to get you out of here.'

'What's that? Why?' Ally struggled to make sense of his words. Connor stirred beside her.

'I've got your bags. You'll have to stay in the clothes you have on. Here's a cup of tea to wake you up.'

Bags? Tea?

'What are you talking about?' Instantly awake, Ally sat up.

'I told you,' Fletcher muttered harshly. 'The river's rising. If we don't get you out of here today, we might be cut off and then you'd be stuck here. We mightn't be able to get you out for weeks. You've got to leave now!'

CHAPTER FOUR

'I CAN'T,' Ally pleaded desperately, her mind in sudden turmoil. 'Fletcher, I can't go now. You want me to look after Connor. You said last night...'

'Obviously,' cut in Fletcher, cocking his head towards the thundering rain outside, 'the situation has changed since last night. Now, please get up. We can't discuss this in here. No need to upset the little guy more than necessary.'

What about upsetting me? Ally fumed as she stumbled out of bed and pulled on her jeans, shivering in the damp morning air. Her turmoil was rapidly consolidating into righteous anger. She glared at Fletcher's stiffened shoulders as she followed him out into the hall. Surely he must know how hurt she felt—to be evacuated without delay or warning! She wasn't a highly contagious patient whose presence threatened the lives of everyone in the vicinity—she was simply in love with him.

Fear twisted to frantic life in her stomach. That was why he had to get rid of her. She was too emotionally threatening.

Ally's heart sank miserably as, looking down the hallway to the scene outside, beyond the huge baskets of ferns hanging from the edge of the veranda, she saw nothing but a wall of thick, grey rain. The drumming on the iron roof continued relentlessly. She shuddered and forced her eyes to return to Fletcher's grim face. But he spun around quickly and his riding boots struck the floorboards loudly as he led her down the polished hall and into his study.

61

As she followed him into the room, Ally considered with a sharp pang of regret, how very little of Fletcher's home she had actually seen. This was clearly his refuge— a pleasantly shabby room with softly glowing timber floors scattered with very old Oriental rugs and timber walls lined with books. There were several low tables piled with his journals, books and newspapers. In the far corner, in front of a red and gold stained-glass window stood his enormous silky oak desk, beside it a narrower table held a computer and fax machine. In the centre of the room clustered a circle of deep, cane lounge chairs lined for comfort with plump, claret-coloured cushions. He gestured for her to sit in one and then drew another closer for himself, chasing a fat ginger tomcat out of it with a distracted shove.

'It's not going to be a pleasant drive,' he said abruptly, and handed her the mug of tea he'd been carrying.

Her mind frozen with despair, she took the mug and noticed how he assiduously avoided any contact with her. She sipped at the tea mechanically, her eyes staring vacantly at the paintings on the opposite wall as she shrugged off the last shreds of sleep and tried to fully take in the grim reality of his news.

'Why not at least wait till it stops raining?' she asked at last. 'Surely unpleasant is an understatement. It's got to be downright dangerous to drive on those narrow dirt tracks through the bush in this weather.'

'We can't wait. It'll be too late. The floodwaters up in the Gulf will link up to the rivers just north of here.'

He hadn't turned on any lamps and in the dim, grey light his eyes were a startling aqua. His gaze locked into hers as he spoke slowly and with exaggerated patience. 'The Fanning River can come up in a matter of hours. And when that happens this property is cut off—caught between the Fanning and the Burdekin rivers—then no one can get out. Sometimes it takes weeks.'

'I'm not a dimwit,' she flashed at him. 'I understood that the first time you told me but, I—I don't mind, Fletch. I'd look after Connor for you. I'd help around...'

'You're going,' Fletcher interrupted gruffly. 'You can't stay. Now don't argue. You don't understand anything about living in the wilderness.'

Wilderness? Ally's eyes wandered around the room, taking in its books and comfortable furniture. Her gaze swung from the vast collection of jazz and classical CDs to the tastefully framed Drysdales and Blackmans hanging around the high-ceilinged, tongue-and-groove walls.

'You have an interesting definition of wilderness,' she responded at last.

He shrugged dismissively. 'Surely after the thousands of kilometres you've travelled—especially the track in from the highway—you must understand how isolated this homestead is. OK, it is a beautiful home. I love it, but it's the only homestead for at least fifty kilometres.'

His sermon was somewhat spoiled by the ginger tom, indignant at being de-throned, jumping onto Ally's lap. She started a little as its tiny claws reached her skin through her denim jeans, but the cat soon settled into a purring, glowing, orange ball beneath her stroking hand.

'What's his name?' she asked, glad of any diversion.

Fletcher stared at her slim fingers as they played with the cat's ears.

'Lightbulb,' he offered, his voice sounding distracted and impatient. 'He's so damn bright, he practically glows in the dark.'

She smiled, but the smile faded as the irony of the situation suddenly struck her. Everyone else was pleased to have her here. Ned Harrison, who saddled the horse for her yesterday, had said as much.

'Sure, you're very welcome' he'd repeated over and over. 'It does a man good to have someone young and pretty about the place. Boss doesn't have...well, anyway, good to see you.'

And Connor certainly needed her. Heaven knows Fletcher didn't know a thing about little children...and Mary and Ned had never been blessed with youngsters. And now even the cat seemed to have taken a fancy to her...

But not Fletcher. Everyone was megahappy for her to stay on Wallaroo Downs except the very man she most wanted to be with in the world. The only man she had ever wanted to be with.

She had sensed from the moment she'd been so roughly woken, that opposition would be pointless, but she couldn't help herself. Last night she'd been silent, but this morning, faced with instant dismissal, she had to keep trying.

'Connor's only just arrived. He doesn't know anybody here. He needs me.'

His face stiffened into hard lines and his eyes were once more fixed on hers with a fierce determination.

'He only got to know you a few days ago. Better that he doesn't get too attached to you, only to lose you again.'

'Lose me? But I wouldn't...'

'Ally, we went over this last night. Of course you won't stay here forever. Please, be sensible about this.' There was a tightness in his face and voice as if he were willing her not to argue—to go quietly.

Well, he could think again! Ally decided as she took another deep swig at the cooling tea. 'Fletcher, I do know what I'm in for here. I told you I haven't lived in Melbourne all my life. I have spent quite a bit of time on cattle properties before. Perhaps you don't realise how well I understand the life. When I was at school, I spent weeks of my holidays every Christmas on Mt. Freedom station with my friend, Roberta Savage and—and I loved it all. I much prefer the bush and the excitement of the cattle yards to the hectic parties and surfing that all my city friends were so crazy about. My parents got quite upset because I'd rather go up to Mt. Freedom in the summer than go to the Gold Coast with them.'

Fletcher listened with narrowed eyes that appeared to be concentrating on the scrolled leaf pattern edging the carpet. 'What you're saying is you've visited properties. There's a big difference between spending a few days in a place and lasting a lifetime.' He paused and Ally felt tiny hairs stand up on the back of her neck. His voice dropped. 'A lifetime. That is what you're talking about, Ally, isn't it?'

'W-what do you m-mean?' The knot in her stomach pulled tighter and her heart pounded as if she'd run a marathon.

Fletcher reached over and ran a gentle hand down her cheek. She felt her skin reddening under its path. His fingers cupped her chin and tilted her face back, but she kept her eyes lowered. She couldn't bear to look into his eyes, to read the truth there.

'Alexandra Fraser,' he said so softly, her name sounded like the title of a love sonnet, 'you've given up your career and you've come with your bags packed. You didn't come all that way just because you wanted a change of scenery.'

She felt a desperate, panicking surge of helplessness, as if she were drowning with no hope of rescue.

'You came because you want to stay here and—' his hand trailed down her neck to her trembling shoulders '—and that's just not going to work.'

A sudden tremor in his voice betrayed his apparent

calm and in the brief moment that their eyes met, Ally read in them sadness and a kind of consternation. Then he turned away, but Ally couldn't accept his words.

A small choking sound erupted in her throat, a mixture of embarrassment and fear. Surely there had been more to their lovemaking in Melbourne than mere sex?

Fletcher had been so passionate and their fiery encounters had been interspersed with long, lingering and sensuous lovemaking, so beautiful she would have been willing to bet everything she possessed that it was real love. And their minds had met, as well. The music, the movies, the food and laughter they'd shared... Even last night, she knew he had been fighting a fundamental longing for her based on something much stronger than the mere urging of hormones.

She jumped to her feet, needing to put some distance between them, and began to pace the floor before him, no longer able to pretend they were having a civilized conversation. There was nothing civilized about the angry hurt that was tearing at her chest.

With both hands, she clutched the mug against her breast.

'You mean you were happy to make love to me in my home in Melbourne, but you don't want me hanging around your place?' she asked, her voice querulous even though her chin jutted forward challengingly.

'That's what I mean.'

He spoke quietly, his eyes fixed, hard, blue stones as he also stood up, towering above her now, regaining all the advantage of height.

Ally's knees almost buckled beneath her, but somehow she managed to hang on to a shred of her rapidly diminishing strength.

'I don't believe you,' she retaliated, her voice matching his quiet tone, her own smoky eyes staring with unflinching directness up into his, even though her heart quailed with fear. 'I'm sorry, Fletcher, but I don't.'

He stood stock-still before her, but his face was very white and a tremor shook his tall frame as if something deep inside fractured.

'What you believe is not really relevant anymore,' he muttered swiftly. 'The fact is we are facing the prospect of a flood which might cut us off from the coast and you have to get off here before that happens—even if I have to pick you up and carry you kicking and squealing.'

A fearful, desperate battle light glinted in Ally's eyes.

'So,' she said softly and evenly, her heart pounding several beats to every carefully delivered syllable, 'you're telling me I can't stay on Wallaroo because you don't love me.'

She ducked her head to hide the quick tears that accompanied those terrible words—words that could bring about the total destruction of everything she believed they had between them. Surely she had pushed things too far, now.

A long, chilling silence was accompanied by the incessant thrumming of the rain.

'That's right.' He sighed as if suddenly very bored with the whole subject. 'I'm so relieved you've finally got the message.'

The mug of tea slipped from her nerveless fingers and crashed on the floorboards between them as Ally reached at the chair's arm for support. Vaguely she was aware of his arms flying around her, holding her steady as her knees collapsed beneath her. His lips were in her hair.

'Ally,' he whispered, 'don't fight me on this, please, please.'

White-faced, trembling, she stared with aversion at the dark hairs springing from the tanned skin of his arm as it tightened around her waist.

'I'm such a fool,' she gasped. 'I had it all wrong.'

His silence offered her no comfort as she stood there sick with horror, but nevertheless leaning against him because she had no strength of her own. She wanted to die. If only she could die now—it would be much easier than facing this awful, awful truth.

'Ally, don't look like that. Ally, you'll be all right. Oh, God, Ally, don't you understand?'

'I don't think I understand anything anymore,' she whispered, tears starting again from beneath reddened eyelids. She gulped back a sob, which clearly almost broke through her self-control, and shook her head. 'I certainly don't understand how you were able to use me the way you did and just cast me aside,' she sniffed, determined not to let the tears fall.

'For God's sake, Ally. I'm sorry about that.'

'Sorry? A-about making love to me?' She wanted to cry so badly. How could she possibly stop herself from bursting into loud, embarrassing sobs?

'Yes. I told you in Melbourne we had no future. I shouldn't have stayed and you shouldn't have come here, Ally. You know I can't resist you. But what you just don't understand is the loneliness, the isolation of this place, the heat, the flies...no concerts, movies, theatres. No fashion worth bothering about out here, for God's sake... You'd miss all that glamour and fame.'

She could not speak to defend herself. The huge swelling in her throat prevented it.

'I can't ask you to put up with it all, Ally. I'm not going to. That's why you have to go.' And he swung away from her, storming for the door. 'I've already put your bags in the back of the Range Rover. In five minutes I'll be back to pick you up. Be ready.'

He disappeared.

Ally ran to the hallway, a lone cry bursting from her,

as she watched his retreating back. She felt she was watching her lifeblood slip away. How tall, broad and unrelenting that back looked as he grabbed an oilskin coat from a hall stand and, raising it to cover his head, disappeared onto the veranda.

Alone. Ally gave in to tears now. He didn't love her. Fletcher didn't love her. Now there was no escaping this shocking reality. She loved Fletcher, wanted him, craved him. He could live on a coral cay in the middle of the Pacific, in Antarctica or on the top of the Himalayas, for all she cared. As long as she could be there, too. She couldn't stop loving him any more than she could will herself to stop breathing.

But he was only interested in her body and even then he could take it or leave it. Right now his only concern was to get rid of her. A loud, agonised sob tore itself from her throat and Ally shoved her hand into her mouth to stop more.

How had it all gone so hopelessly wrong? How could she have been such a lovesick fool clinging to a useless dream?

She stumbled down the hall towards the veranda, but came to a hasty, frozen stop in the doorway. Fletcher hadn't left; he was still leaning on the railing near the top of the steps, his face buried in his hands, his shoulders slumped in exhaustion.

As Ally stared, bewildered, Fletcher gave a groan and she quickly stepped back out of sight, her heart thudding painfully in her chest.

But, as if he sensed her there, he suddenly straightened quickly and jumped the few steps from the low veranda before striding off into the rain.

She closed her eyes in confusion. Clearly he didn't feel quite as offhand about all this as he pretended. But, in a few short minutes she would be leaving, never to see Fletcher again. If only she could hate him!

She forced her stiff legs back to Connor's bedroom to take one last look at him. Amazingly, he was still asleep. Obviously, the long journey from Sydney had exhausted him more than she realised and the continuous beat of the rain had definite lullaby qualities. His little body looked smaller than ever in the middle of the big white bed, his eyelashes lying softly against cheeks that were warm and pink with sleep. Damp, dark curls of hair lay flattened against the side of his head.

He was such a sweet little boy.

Although she had only just started to get to know him, already he tugged at her emotionally in a way that her nephew and nieces, her sister's children, didn't. He seemed so vulnerable, so innocent and alone, so needing of love.

She wanted to kiss him goodbye, but was afraid he would wake and she couldn't bear to have to explain why she was going.

'I hope they look after you,' she whispered. 'I'll miss you, sweetheart.'

There was a step in the doorway behind her. Fletcher was there, standing dark and stern in his dripping coat. He indicated with a jerk of his head that she should leave. Kissing her fingers, she dropped them to the pillow beside the little head, turned and stepped quietly away.

'Put this on,' he said, handing her a coat as she joined him outside the room.

'Who's going to look after him now?' she asked.

'Mary Harrison. I've spoken to her.'

'I thought she was too busy.'

'Don't start that again, Ally. As I said, things have changed. She's an adaptable woman. She'll cope. There's no mustering now with all this rain, so she'll have time.'

'She's a good bush woman, I take it,' Ally replied through gritted teeth as she shrugged her arms into the coat he held for her.

'Exactly,' Fletcher replied, and his lips closed over the word with a definite air of finality.

'But I need to tell her about Connor, about his needs...'

'Why?' Fletcher asked, looking at her with widened, wary eyes. 'He's not ill, is he? Not on medication?'

'No, nothing like that. But he's still very frightened of loud noises and he has one favourite story he must hear every night before he goes to sleep...'

'Did you bring it with you?'

'Yes, of course. It's on his bedside table.'

'And it's called?'

'Where is my mother?'

The shock was clearly evident on Fletcher's face. 'That's a bit morbid, isn't it? Considering what happened to his own mother?'

'I know,' Ally replied. 'That's what I thought at first, but he insisted. It was the only story that would settle him. But...' She looked away from him, twisting her hands nervously. 'You see, whenever I read it to him I change the ending. He can't read and he seems quite satisfied...'

'What do you mean?'

'Well, I...I thought Connor should be helped to accept the truth...that sometimes we can't find our mothers any-more...so, in the story, when I get to the part where the little bird finally finds his mother, I change it so that he doesn't find her, but instead he finds a—a godfather.'

From under her thick, dark lashes, she shot him a quick glance. He was staring back silent and still as a statue. She continued. 'Connor was very pleased with the idea.

And he is so happy now that he has found his own god-father.' She forced herself to smile at him.

White-lipped, Fletcher continued to stare at her for an-other long, difficult moment and then he spun on his heel and marched towards the waiting car.

'Let's go.'

Once she was in the vehicle, there was no chance for backward farewell glances at the homestead. With an an-gry firing of the motor, the Range Rover leapt into the grey wall of rain, its windscreen wipers valiantly trying to clear a small glimpse of the muddy, slippery-looking track ahead.

'Is having to delay the muster a problem?' Ally asked tentatively, straining her voice to reach Fletcher over the roar of the engine, the clatter of the wipers and the drum-ming of the rain all around them. Her attempt at conver-sation was met by a grunt. Fletcher's concentration was focused on the steering wheel and the road ahead. After only a night's rain, the track was already starting to wash away in places and it was littered with fallen branches. As the car swerved to avoid one of these, Ally was thrown sideways onto Fletcher's arm. Her head ended up resting on his shoulder—a hard and unyielding shoulder from which she flinched back quickly.

'Put your seat belt on,' he barked. 'It's going to be a rough ride. Can't be helped.'

It didn't feel as if she could actually be leaving Wallaroo Downs. Firstly, she'd hardly seen anything of the place and secondly, the journey was too hazardous, too much like some wild adventure, to be concluded by simply dumping her at a bus station, but that was what she assumed Fletcher had planned.

As if reading her thoughts, he spoke. 'With a bit of luck we'll get to Townsville before dark. You can fly to Melbourne direct from there.'

'You're taking me all that way to the coast?'

'Only a few hours once we get on the highway.'

'You want to make sure I get completely out of the district, don't you?'

This was met by a silence, which unnerved Ally and sent her voice shooting several decibels higher. 'You're scared I'll come sneaking back and make a nuisance of myself.'

'Don't get hysterical.'

'Hysterical?' *Hysterical?* This time Ally couldn't help herself. After the remarkable restraint she'd exercised all morning, there was no way she was going to be accused of hysteria! How dare the man! Maybe she *could* hate him! 'I think I'm behaving with admirable calm and decorum. One thing you don't have to be afraid of is that I'll come scurrying back halfway across the nation to throw myself at you again.'

'Hell.'

'What's the matter?' It only took a split second for Ally to realise that Fletcher hadn't been listening to her pathetic little tirade. The vehicle had come to a sudden stop and his eyes were fixed on the road ahead where it dipped steeply away from the ridge on which they were poised. Ally peered through the rain to see what had caused them to stop.

It was difficult to see more than a few metres of the gravel road ahead, but the track looked more like a creek, as streams of swirling brown water rushed down to meet more water below. It was then she realised what had happened. The road disappeared into the river.

'The blasted Fanning's up already,' muttered Fletcher, jamming on the hand brake and cutting the engine.

'Is that the river washing across the road?' asked Ally lamely.

'Across the bridge, damn it. It's only a low concrete

bridge, no sides or anything, but it serves us through most wets. This water must have come already from the head-waters up in the Gulf. It's been raining up there all week.'
Ally stared at the frothing, muddy flood rushing below them. The current was obviously very strong, but she had no idea how deep the water was. Surely Fletcher would not attempt to drive through it, even in a four-wheel-drive vehicle?

He opened his car door.

'Where are you going?'

'Having a closer look. Stay in the car,' he ordered with maddening abruptness.

With gritted teeth Ally watched as his dark-cloaked figure strode down the incline towards the water. It was impossible to see through the windscreen, so she wound down the window beside her and stuck her head into the rain. A metre or so away from the water's swirling edge Fletcher paused, hands on hips, staring ahead of him. Then slowly he began to take off his coat and roll it up before placing it next to a nearby boulder.

'What are you doing?' she screamed through the rain as he began to walk towards the swirling torrent.

'Testing the water. Stay there!'

Not likely, Ally muttered to herself as she shoved open the door on her side.

'Fletcher, don't be ridiculous!' she called as she raced down the slope towards him. Her coat flapped open and her head and shirtfront were quickly drenched, but it hardly mattered if Fletcher had taken leave of his senses. The creek seethed, the mud-brown torrent hurling itself forward at suicidal speed. 'You're not going in there?' she panted as she reached him. He scowled back at her.

'Calm down, Ally. I know what I'm doing. It's not wise to drive through floodwaters till you've tested them out first on foot.'

'Oh, and that's really wise, isn't it? Fletcher, please, don't go in there. It looks dreadfully dangerous.'

'I doubt it's more than knee deep.'

Ally bit back another retort. Fletcher glared at her, his eyes dark blue slits and his heavy overnight stubble outlined a determined jaw. It wasn't difficult to read his thoughts. He knew this environment, this land. She was only a city slicker and a female to boot. With an exasperated sigh she shrugged and gestured for him to go about his manly business.

Fletcher stepped forward purposefully, his elastic-sided riding boots disappearing somewhere below the brown, swiftly flowing stream. One step, two, three. Ally supposed she should be pleased that he'd been right. The water wasn't deep. A good few centimetres of jeans below his knees were still dry. He turned and winked, flashing her a cheeky grin that made her insides melt. But she couldn't force a return smile. Each dangerous step he took dealt a humiliating blow to her battered self-esteem. His desperation to get rid of her meant he would risk his life rather than have her stay with him indefinitely!

He was nearing the middle of the wide stretch of water and now it was above his knees, but only just. A sudden swift surge in the current buffeted him a little, making him sidestep to retain his balance and Ally gasped, hardly aware of her hands clasped tightly together as if in prayer. She couldn't stop herself caring for him, fearing for his safety…loving him, even in the face of his outright rejection. This useless love was a burden she would have to carry to her grave. She bit her lip painfully as she watched him stand still and feel the ground below him carefully with one foot. Then slowly he edged forward again.

Something dark snaked its way into the corner of her

vision. A tree branch was hurtling along in the whipping water.

'Look out!' she screamed.

Fletcher turned and she caught the quick flicker of concern, which tightened his features as he tried to step backwards, out of the way. Too late!

'Fletcher!' Horrified, Ally watched the tree branch ram into him. Then in dread she saw his knees buckle as he was swept away by its force. 'Oh, no! Oh, God!' She ran towards the water, but already Fletcher's dark head was all she could see and a split second later it was disappearing around a bend as he was dragged off by the savage current.

Sobbing, Ally stumbled through the still streaming rain along the slippery bank. Where was he? All she could see was disgusting, ugly brown water rushing headlong as if possessed. Surely it was faster now than when they first stopped.

'Fletch! Oh, Fletcher!' She ran on, oblivious to scratches and stumbles, her eyes riveted to the swirling mass, desperate for that dear, dark shape of his head. Just when she thought she could see it, it would disappear again. It was so difficult to see anything through all the dratted rain. Suddenly she let out a yelp as she lurched into something sharp. It was barbed wire. A fence line was running down the slope and across the river, disappearing underwater at the centre.

Her eyes scanned its length. There he was! Caught against the barbed wire! Thank heavens. He was moving, trying it seemed, to untangle himself. The water would be pinning him unmercifully against the sharp barbs. But maybe he'd be able to pull himself along the fence and back to safety.

'Can you follow the fence?' she yelled.

'I'm stuck!' There were more words but the wind

whipped them away. Stuck! His clothes must be wound around the wire somehow, imprisoning him. Ally closed her eyes as a sickening wave of fear engulfed her. There was nothing else for her to do but to go in after him.

CHAPTER FIVE

IT WAS just as well Ally hadn't tried to sound heroic when she called back to Fletcher above the thunder of the water, for her words trailed off in the wind. But Fletcher must have heard, because as she raised a tentative boot to step into the flood, she heard him roar back.

'Stop!'

Feeling guiltily relieved, she paused. With luck she might not have to go in the flooded river. Perhaps he'd already freed himself and was about to make his way back along the fence. Standing on tiptoes, she peered at the spot midstream where she had last seen him, and her heart leapt to her throat. He had disappeared! And when she checked the fence line, he wasn't making his way along that, either. All she could see was the wide stretch of racing, evil water.

Sheer panic clutched her chest in a vicelike grip. Fletcher drowned?

Drowned while attempting to escort her off his property? Drowned because she had forced her love onto him when he had not asked for or wanted it. Because she'd chased after him with the same pig-headed determination that had been her lifelong trademark—to achieve whatever goal she'd set before herself.

Mesmerised by the swirling, coffee-coloured flood, Ally was unable to think past her guilt, and she felt the weight of it pour over her and flood into her veins, as if she, too, were drowning.

Then at last, right where he had been before, she caught sight of Fletcher's dark head as it popped to the surface and she understood that he'd been trying to free something caught down low. It was only when a loud sob broke from her lips she realised she'd been holding her breath.

She waited to see if he was now free to move, but it looked unlikely. In fact he looked as if he hardly had the strength to cling to the fence and hold himself above the water. Dragging off her coat, which she knew would be a hindrance in the current, Ally took a deep breath.

'Hold on, Fletcher,' she called. And this time there was no protest.

I don't know if I'm strong enough for this, she thought as she plunged into the swirling current. The first few steps were easy enough except that every time she grabbed a fresh hold on the barbed wire, she felt its stinging jab. But as she moved into knee-deep water, the force of the current kept slamming her slender frame against the fence, which ripped and tore her clothes and flesh. There was also the added danger that she, too, would become trapped and tangled up in the hideous wire but she kept on, each step more difficult.

Her arms ached from holding her body out from the wire as the swiftly eroding riverbed kept shifting beneath her feet. She was very tired. At any moment she would be out of her depth and there was no way she could hold herself upright then. I'm no use to Fletcher at all, she thought wretchedly.

'Ally, hold it! I'm OK. Go back.'

As his beautiful, authoritative command reached her, every terrified nerve in her body sang with relief. She would give anything to go back. But when she looked towards the bank, the return journey looked as bad as that still ahead. The thought of dragging one foot behind the other in either direction was almost too much.

'Ally, stop. I'm free.'

Although she couldn't see much past the wet hair plastered on her face and the swirling waters all around her, she could make out Fletcher's dark shape working his way along the wire. 'My boot was caught, but I got it off,' he called. 'Hold on, I'm coming.'

Eagerly she tugged sodden lumps of hair away from her eyes to see better. With his strong arms, Fletcher was holding himself off the barbs as he edged towards her. And he actually had the audacity to be grinning at her, his brilliant blue eyes the only spots of colour in the murky river.

At the sight of him free again, no longer depending on her to rescue him, Ally's courage and strength seemed to falter. The force of the chest-high water became almost impossible to withstand and the horrid brown tide pinned her relentlessly to the barbed wire.

She struggled to lift herself away from the wire and move back to the bank. She couldn't fail now and force Fletcher to rescue her on top of his own exhaustion. It became of the utmost importance to stop thinking about how every part of her body was bruised or cut or exhausted.

The distance to the bank looked impossible now. How had she crossed it before? She willed her hands and feet to continue moving in spite of the cruel pressure of the current.

It didn't work.

'Ally.' Fletcher's voice was much closer. She would have answered back if she had sufficient leftover energy. Another step. And another. Her ankle wobbled dangerously beneath her. She couldn't, mustn't slip.

But she did.

Rushing muddy water filled her mouth and she spluttered and coughed as she was raised briefly by the force of the water and thrown again onto the barbed wire. Her head grazed the timber fence post. But before she could grab it, once more she slipped down into the filthy rushing stream. She couldn't find the strength to fight. It was too much. She tried vainly to struggle to the surface, but in the black, murky depths she could hardly tell where it was. Grabbing frantically for the wire, she no longer felt the stinging, ripped skin. Surely she could pull herself up? If only she could breathe!

Something grabbed her shirt collar. She was being lifted. Bursting above the surface of the water, she gulped and coughed and gasped and spluttered.

'Woo-a, Ally, you'll be all right, now. Just breathe, slowly and deeply.'

Fletcher was holding her. God, she wasn't going to die after all. She sank against him. Lovely Fletcher. She would thank him if she didn't need all her precious energy just to keep breathing.

Her head resting against his chest, she felt for a moment that she could stay there forever, sleep perhaps. In the safety of Fletcher's arms, she hardly noticed the murky water rushing around her.

'Come on, let's get moving,' Fletcher said close to her ear. Move? Did she have to? She tried to reach out to the wire, ready to haul herself forward, but two strong hands tightened around her hips and raised her up. 'Just as well you're only little—as light as a feather,' he grunted as he lifted her above the water level. Instinctively she tucked her legs up, realising that it would be much easier for him to carry her above rather than through the current. He slowly made his way to the bank holding her high. Ally felt her lips curl into a smile. Wonderful Fletcher.

Almost near the edge, he stumbled a little and lowered her quickly into the ankle-deep water.

'Sorry.' He smiled crookedly. 'A little woozy. I think I gave my head a pretty hard whack on that fence post.'

'You've a nasty red gash on your temple.' Ally reached up to gently touch the side of his forehead.

'It'll keep,' he sighed. Then he smiled down at her. 'Thanks for coming to my rescue.'

Ally shook her head. 'Fat lot of good it did. I was about as much help as…as a fashion designer in a flood.'

Fletcher threw back his head and laughed at her weak joke and then he winced, his hand flying swiftly to his temple. Ally frowned. Clearly he'd had a very nasty blow. They should get out of the water.

'Hey, I was so wet I hadn't noticed. The rain's stopped. Let's get out of here.' She took Fletcher's hand and stepped towards the bank, but he drew her gently back to him, enclosing her in his arms, both of them dripping wet.

'I meant it, passionfruit.'

'What's that?' she murmured huskily.

'Thank you for coming to my rescue.' His kisses were surprisingly warm on her cold cheek. 'It was madness, of course, but very brave.'

'I was so frightened. I thought you were going to drown,' she whispered, noticing how weary he looked and how much the escapade had taken out of him. His normally tanned face was pale and his eyes were underlined by deep shadows, emphasising his exhaustion.

'But you still came after me, even though you were frightened. You're such a gutsy little thing.' He grinned, his lips grazing hers teasingly.

She didn't dare ask the questions that whirled desperately in her head about what would happen now that they couldn't cross the river. Instead she smiled.

'Perhaps I earned my first points as a bush woman?'

His thumb outlined her jaw and trailed up to circle an

earlobe. 'You know,' he said gently, 'even when you look like a drowned rat, you're ravishing.'

Ally knew then that she would not get the answer she wanted. She consoled herself by leaning into Fletcher's strength, parting her lips to meet his.

His stubble grazed her chin, but its scratchiness didn't bother her, just as her stinging cut skin and the floodwater still swirling round her ankles hardly registered. She didn't notice anything but Fletcher's kiss, which deepened as his hands slid down to her buttocks and held her tightly against him. She could no longer remember that she had thought it unwise for them to stay there in the water rather than get dry and warm again.

With his tongue seeking out the velvet softness of her mouth, she surrendered completely to the heady sensations he always aroused in her. She shifted her body even closer to his, wanting to feel all of him. She could hear herself moaning softly, melting as she always did under Fletcher's overwhelming, seductive power. Reaching her hands to the sides of his head to hold his face against her own, she felt something warm and sticky. She gasped. It was blood. And it was streaming out of the wound on Fletcher's forehead.

'Fletch, we've got to do something about this. It looks bad.'

He released her reluctantly. They both stepped the few short paces to the bank. And then Fletcher collapsed. Swaying briefly beside her like a weakened tree in a storm, he lurched forward to become a crumpled heap in the mud.

'Fletch!!' Ally dropped frantically to her knees. He looked so deathly pale, so still and—lifeless. Panic seized her. She kissed his cold cheek, his lips—no, surely, surely not? She looked at his chest, appalled. Was it rising and falling? Was he breathing? At first, in panic she could see no movement. But, no, there it was. Thank God he was alive.

So, she told herself, he had fainted. It was important to stay calm—simply a matter of getting him to the truck and back to Wallaroo homestead, to help.

Simply? Ally swallowed the dryness in her throat.

'Fletch, why are you so damned big!' she sighed as she tried to lift him up the bank. Even as she was making laborious progress away from the water's edge, his feet, one without a boot, dragging behind, Ally's mind raced ahead to her next task. She knew it would be almost impossible. There was no way she could lift an unconscious Fletcher up into the elevated cabin of the Range Rover, built for high clearance on rough bush terrain.

'I'll have to leave you here and go for help,' she whispered. 'Sorry, Fletch. I'll get your coat and mine and wrap you up. At least it's not raining anymore.' With a flash of inspiration from a distant first aid class, she rolled him onto his side into the recovery position. Then she dropped another flurry of kisses on his unresponsive cheek and dashed to find the coats.

As she tucked them around him, her determination almost failed her. She couldn't just leave him alone out here. Big, strong, mountainous Fletcher looked so vulnerable, lying inactive on the muddy bank. His face was white and the contrasting harsh red wound on his forehead alarmed her so that she almost gave in to tears.

But she had to go.

She kissed him again, felt his pulse, which was steady and then, with a supreme effort of will, forced herself to head off.

To her surprise, the Range Rover was no more difficult to drive than her own small city sedan. Now that the rain had stopped, she could see the track quite clearly and the power steering enabled her to dodge fallen branches quite expertly, while the huge tyres gripped the slippery surface safely. By the time she reached Wallaroo Downs, Mary and Ned were already at the front steps, clearly puzzled that the vehicle should be returning so soon.

'Fletcher's had an accident down at the creek,' she sobbed as soon as the engine died. 'He's too heavy for me to lift, but we should get back quickly in case he wakes and tries to walk somewhere.'

'I'll take the tray-backed utility,' shouted Ned. 'It'll be easier to put him in the back. Mary, you ring the Flying Doctor and find out how far away he is. Come with me, Miss.'

In no time at all they were skidding back down the track.

'I left Fletcher on the bank to the right, just near where the fence runs down across the creek.'

'You should have used the CB radio. There's one in the Range Rover. Then you could have stayed with him.'

Ally felt very foolish. She hadn't even thought of a radio, let alone looked for one. And anyway, she wouldn't have had the first idea how to use it. Perhaps Fletcher was right. It seemed that in the bush she was only a nuisance.

'Oh, heavens, he's got to still be there,' she prayed.

He was. In fact, to Ally, who leapt out of the vehicle before it had completely stopped, and dropped to her knees beside the dark shape on the ground, it looked as if he hadn't moved at all since she left. He was still pale and unconscious, but breathing.

'Fletch,' she cried, lifting his cold hand in both hers. She kissed it, rubbing her face against his palm in an effort to warm it. 'Ned, what do you think?' she called as the stockman hobbled stiffly towards them.

'Well, he's out to it all right. Colour's not too bad. You think anything could be broken?'

'No, no limbs or anything,' she replied, remembering how easily Fletcher had carried her through the swift current. 'But I think he's been knocked out by a blow on the head. Look here.' Gently she turned Fletcher's head to reveal the deep, red wound. A soft moan drifted from his lips.

Ned nodded. 'Right. Then we just have to get him back and let the doc have a look at him.'

Ned had lowered the tailgate on the utility, and between the two of them, using Fletcher's strong, oiled canvas coat as a stretcher, they were able to lift him into the back and settle him on some old sugar bags on the floor.

'I'll stay with Fletcher,' she said, sitting cross-legged beside him on the floor of the ute's tray back and tucking a coat under his head.

'Good idea,' Ned remarked. 'Hang on tight, won't you?'

She was grateful that he had warned her, because as the truck took off, Ally only just had time to grab the sides for support. She found it easiest to kneel and hold Fletcher's head steady between her knees, as she needed both hands to brace herself against all the bumps, even though Ned was taking it quite slowly.

Around and above them, tall eucalypts, wattles and paperbarks dripped quietly, but beyond the treetops, the sky still loomed dark, burdened with heavy, black clouds. There would soon be more rain.

The trip back was slower than the other journeys and Ally was sick with anxiety by the time the low, iron roof and bull-nosed front veranda could be glimpsed between the huge tamarind trees in front of the Wallaroo homestead.

She looked down at Fletcher and longed for the life to spring back into his features. He still looked quite superb, but it was distressing to see that strong, powerful face lying still and slack. Even if he opened his eyes and told her to get lost, she would at least know he was all right.

'Here we are. Home safe and sound,' she murmured to his inert, quiet body. His eyelids fluttered and she bent low, eagerly kissing his cheek, his brow, his lips. 'Oh, Fletch, wake up, wake up,' she urged. She fancied his lips curved into a smile and she kissed them again.

'Beautiful,' she thought she heard him whisper.

Above, she heard the put-put-put sound of a motor in the air.

'Chopper's coming,' called Ned as he jumped from the truck's cabin. 'Probably been roped in to take him to hospital in the Towers. Flying Doctor's plane wouldn't be able to land in this weather. It's wet enough to bog a duck. He'll be right now, love,' he added as he patted Ally's shoulder. She was still crouched low beside Fletcher. 'No sweat. They'll have him back on deck quick as a flash. Not the first time this bloke's copped a dong on the head. You wait and see, he'll bounce back cheekier than ever.'

Ned kept up the comforting patter all the time the helicopter circled above the homestead and then slowly settled to land in the home paddock about a hundred metres away.

'I'll drive 'im over nice and slow, now,' Ned said gently as he swung back into the cabin. 'We'll look after him, love. Perhaps you could go and tell my missus to put a cuppa on for us.'

Ally knew she was being dismissed. There was no more she could do. And as she had no claim on Fletcher she could hardly insist on flying to Charters Towers with him. It wasn't as if she was next of kin or anything. She was merely the girl who'd brought Fletcher's godson up from the city. With tear-filled eyes she watched the utility drive carefully and slowly away and she could see the dark bulky outline of Fletcher lying in the back. All alone.

It was over a week before the helicopter brought Fletcher back. A long, frightening time during which those waiting at the homestead received patchy telephone messages from the hospital. He regained consciousness the day after the accident, but there were complications. X-rays and tests took up the next few days while Ally nervously paced the verandas at Wallaroo and the rain returned fiercer and more monotonous than ever. She kept herself as busy as possible with Connor, reading to him, drawing and singing with him; playing with the many toys they had brought from Sydney.

She helped Mary about the huge house and, with Connor, took over some of the chores such as feeding the chickens and weeding the kitchen garden which, though waterlogged at present, would thrive once the rainwater drained away. But always, dominating everything else, was Fletcher. Her fear for his condition consumed her so that she couldn't eat or sleep, and during the day a restless energy kept her continually on the move, never able to rest.

Finally, more news came through one afternoon when Ally had joined Mary and Ned for afternoon tea in the cheery, old-fashioned kitchen. Mary came hurrying away from the phone to tell Ally and Ned the news as they sat at the old scrubbed pine table. Fletcher was going to be all right, but he had amnesia.

'Amnesia?' queried Ned. 'Like last time?'

Panic ripped through Ally like a flaming arrow. She stared at Ned in horror.

'Yes,' nodded his wife, her shiny sunburnt face looking solemn. 'Apparently this accident shook up his old wound again.' She noticed Ally's white, puzzled face and added for her benefit, 'Fletcher had a bad fall from a horse a few years back when he was riding at the Mingela Rodeo—lost his memory for about a month until it all healed up.'

'He forgot everything?' asked Ally, her mind reeling, her heart racketing around wildly at the news. Somehow, the thought of big, handsome Fletcher losing his grip on the past frightened her terribly.

'No, not everything. It was funny really. It was only things that had happened recent like that he forgot—for about six months back—but he could remember who he was and who we were and how to run a cattle property and everything important like that.' Mary grinned as she lifted the enormous blue teapot and poured her husband another cup of tea. 'Of course he couldn't remember the accident or which bills were owing...but in time it all came back right as rain.'

'And that's what he's got again, is it?' Ned asked as he took his big mug of tea between two huge hands.

'Seems so,' said Mary. She looked at Ally quizzically. 'I suppose he mightn't remember you, love.'

'Perhaps not,' whispered Ally, and fresh panic leapt into her chest so that she could hardly breathe. If Fletcher did not know her, what could that mean? If he'd forgotten meeting her, their time together in Melbourne...?

'Does he know about Connor?' she heard herself ask.

'Plenty of time to explain to him about that,' interrupted Ned. 'One shock at a time will be enough for now.'

But by the time Fletcher returned, there had been several long telephone conversations with Ned and he'd been brought pretty much up to date. He knew about the floods and that the mustering had to be delayed and he also knew that he was now legal guardian of his godson and that the boy had arrived with his nanny and was well settled in.

But that was all he knew.

The days were agony for Ally. It seemed terrible that she couldn't talk to Fletcher, couldn't hear his voice for herself, but the Harrisons never invited her to the phone and she could hardly insist. One night, when they had retired to their own little cottage several hundred metres away, she walked to the telephone standing on the front hall table and very nearly rang the hospital and asked to speak to him. But, as she stood there, her trembling hand poised above the receiver, practising what she would say, the futility of it all sank in.

She could picture Fletcher sitting in his starched, white hospital bed, holding the phone to his ear, listening to her patchwork explanation, his features clouded by a look of total disbelief. What was she going to say if he didn't remember her? If he had no idea who she was, how could she begin to explain why she had rung? She could hardly tell him, 'I'm your lover. We are one very hot item together. I thought you might like to know.'

She walked away from the phone; her shoulders slumped with disappointment and her hands hanging limply by her sides.

Perhaps when he saw her again, he would know as soon as he looked at her that they had a very special relationship. But what if he didn't? How could she bear it if Fletcher treated her with the complete indifference of a stranger?

Now, her real torment began. During the day she could usually occupy herself to a degree by entertaining Connor, but the nights were agony. For hours she would lie, twisting her thoughts into tortuous knots as she tried to imagine meeting Fletcher all over again.

Would he know her? If he did, would he send her

packing straight away? If...if... What if...? Could she bring herself to leave now, when she had begun to feel so at home here? She had spent the days familiarising herself with every nook and cranny of the homestead where Fletcher had spent his whole life. It was a huge and beautiful old home and she was beginning to love it almost as much as its master.

'Stop fretting. He'll be all right, love,' Ned would reassure her when she appeared, her eyes ringed by dark circles in the morning. 'He's the strongest man I know and I've met lots of tough men in the bush. And he's the best,' he muttered with a sincere smile. 'They surely got the recipe right when they made that man. But then again, it's high time he had someone pretty to worry about him,' he added with a knowing smirk.

By the afternoon Fletcher was due to return, the rain had stopped and Ally had hung some washing for herself and Connor on the clothesline, which stretched from the ancient mango tree in the yard behind the homestead. Mary had been quite agitated, insisting that washing wasn't a part of a nanny's duties, but Ally needed to keep busy. She was far too nervous to sit still. Even washing wasn't really enough activity to calm her tense, fluttering stomach.

She put Connor to rest with Shy, his platypus, and a few favourite books on a daybed on the screened back veranda where he could enjoy a sleep in the fresh air.

Apart from her frantic nervousness, she was feeling happy at the thought of seeing Fletcher again. The day was clear and fresh after the rain and she took time during Connor's nap to shower and change into clean jeans and a simple white linen shirt—one of her own designs. She tied her dark shiny hair back from her face with a deep violet satin ribbon, so that without make-up her clear,

fresh complexion was displayed in stark contrast to her
dark hair.

It was as she was unpegging a row of Connor's striped
socks that the helicopter engine erupted once again in the
sky above her. She looked up and saw the metallic mon-
ster glinting in the sun as it circled above, dropping
closer. Ally felt her already high anxiety levels increase
dramatically. As the helicopter swooped across the
clothesline, sending the clothes dancing from the blades'
down draught, she could see Fletcher sitting in the front
seat, dark and handsome as ever, staring down at her. In
an instant he was gone, over the homestead roof to land
on the broad run of lawn out the front, but that brief
glimpse had been enough.

He had stared at her with a puzzled frown creasing his
broad forehead. There had been no sign of recognition.

She suddenly felt sick, her body chilled, almost numb.
Hastily she dragged the rest of the washing from the line,
her heart racing frantically. By the time she'd thrust the
last of the clothes in the wicker basket, she was trembling
violently. It had been bad enough when Fletcher had
wanted to send her away, but at least then, there had
always been Melbourne, and their special week could
somehow remain a tenuous bond, a fragile link she would
always have with him whatever else happened. But now,
if their past had been wiped out, erased from his mind
as surely as if they had never met, he would treat her
like a complete stranger and she wondered if she could
bear it.

She rushed across the lawn, dumped the washing basket on the veranda, and swept up Connor. She had no
idea where she would take him, but one thing was certain; she had to get out of the house. She couldn't line
up with Mary and Ned as part of the reception committee
welcoming back the master.

'Let's go for a walk,' she said, forcing herself to sound bright and enthusiastic. 'There's a nice track going down to the creek.'

'OK,' responded Connor happily. Fortunately he was a child who wakened easily and he was always ready for an adventure. Ally tied up his sneakers quickly and was soon rapidly making her way away from the house and towards the line of trees at the far end of the paddock.

They were halfway across the sweep of paddock when the helicopter took off again and Connor looked up waving excitedly. The pilot saw him and waved back and even leaned forward to take a closer look at them both.

Of course they couldn't get down to the creek. It was still in flood and the track was washed out in several places. Ally realised guiltily that Fletcher had probably never retrieved his trail bike from where he'd abandoned it the day she arrived and by now it would probably be swept away. Fletcher wouldn't even be able to remember what had happened to it unless she told him, she thought with a painful stab of remorse.

'Perhaps we'd better go back after all,' she said, eyeing the muddied track. 'It's about afternoon teatime,' she added in case Connor protested. And the promise of milk and Mary's Anzac biscuits was enough to turn him around without once questioning Ally's contrariness.

I guess I'll just have to face the music, she thought nervously as they retraced their steps across the paddock. But when they reached the homestead, her courage failed her and she pushed Connor forward towards the kitchen.

'You go on in and find Mary and she'll give you your afternoon tea and you'll be able to see Uncle Fletcher, too,' she said, giving him a gentle shove towards the passage, which led to the kitchen. Connor looked at her with wide-eyed curiosity.

'What about you?' he asked.

'I'll...I'll be along later,' she said. 'I've got a few things to do. I need to fold the washing.'

'OK.' Connor smiled at her and obediently trotted off.

Flustered, desperately anxious in case she saw Fletcher at any moment, Ally snatched up the basket of clothes and headed to the far end of the long veranda. She almost stopped to work there at the little table where she and Connor often occupied themselves, but then she decided it was still too visible, so she continued on to her own room and began to fold the clothes frantically, setting them out on little piles on her bed.

The folding was almost finished when she heard firm, deliberate footsteps marching along the veranda. They had to be Fletcher's. Ned's arthritis caused him to walk with a limp and Mary shuffled around quietly in slippers that were kind to her bunions. Was he coming to find her?

Ally stiffened, fear prickling her spine while Lightbulb curled comfortably in the middle of the bed and swished his tail lazily. Her palms grew sweaty and she pressed them together as she stood rigid with tension, her back to the door. She caught her reflection in the oval mirror on the opposite wall. Her pale, wide-eyed face framed by a bell of dark hair looked so vulnerable. If only she could look more sophisticated and sexy—or at least more in control. The steps grew closer and Ally saw an embarrassing tide of blushing pink sweep up her neck and into her cheeks.

Then a shadow fell across the bed as she sensed a tall form block the doorway and a familiar, deep voice drawled, 'So this is the nanny's hide-out.'

CHAPTER SIX

STAY calm! Ally warned herself as she turned around slowly. Fletcher stood in the doorway with a piece of sticking plaster high on his temple, the only evidence that he'd had an accident.

He was smiling at her with a devastating twinkle in his blue eyes. Her heart seemed to stop beating and a painful jolt tightened her chest so that she had difficulty breathing. He looked for all the world as if he were waiting for her to run into his arms and welcome him back.

But of course he wasn't and she couldn't. He didn't know her. His smile was simply the same charming grin he used to dazzle any mere mortal who crossed his path. There was no underlying message, no hidden flash of understanding, no shared memories.

He had absolutely no idea who she was.

'How do you do?' he said, extending a strong, brown hand. 'I believe we have met, but I'm afraid I need to start over again.' He grinned once more, his eyes sparkling at her and his smile warm enough to melt her bones.

'Hello.'

It was an inadequate response, but it was the best she could muster. She stood almost shivering under his curious gaze, while in contrast, her cheeks continued to blaze relentlessly.

He leant a broad shoulder casually against the doorframe and folded his arms across his chest, so that Ally's attention was drawn to his powerful, tanned forearms. She found herself taking in every detail—the black, finely knit polo shirt tucked into tailored grey slacks, his damp and neatly combed hair and smooth, clean-shaven jaw. He looked wonderful. Just as sexy as he did in his everyday jeans, cotton shirts and riding boots or, in a tux, as he'd been when she had first met him at the show.

Doing her best not to be overawed by his physical presence, Ally carefully composed her features to seem unimpressed and calm, but of course she was neither. Fletcher had been gone for ages and her whole face felt as if it was beaming ridiculously with the sheer joy of having him so near again. It was as if now that he was back, the world was spinning safely on its axis once more. She could look forward to each day following the next.

It was a foolish reaction really, for she knew that as soon as Fletcher's memory returned he would be just as angry as he'd been before and he would send her packing. He was only being charming because he didn't know who she was.

His eyes slid politely over her and then narrowed as he quickly scanned the room and her belongings. 'I see you've settled in. That's good. Are you comfortable?'

'Oh, yes. I'm very comfortable, thank you. You have a very lovely home.'

He shrugged. 'Yes, it's not bad, is it? It's been in the family for over a century. My great-grandfather was one of the first settlers in the district.'

I know! Ally wanted to reply. You told me all about this home, about your life, when we were in Melbourne.

She turned away awkwardly to hide her hurt and bent to stack Connor's folded clothes. As she straightened, her eyes met his, reflected in the mirror. She could have sworn he'd been staring at her behind. An unbidden pulse began to race. Their eyes met in the mirror and he grinned again, sheepishly.

'Er...I was wondering,' he said, actually having the grace to sound uncomfortable. 'Did I hire you?'

A surge of guilt prickled in Ally's chest. For a woman who had spent weeks planning and scheming her arrival on Wallaroo Downs, her preparation for Fletcher's return from hospital lacked foresight. She really should have spent more time considering how she was going to handle all his unanswerable questions. Instead, she'd wasted all her emotion on missing him and hadn't even begun to consider the complications she would now have to deal with on a day-to-day basis.

There was no option really. If she tried to be anything except the hired help, she would face probing questions that would only lead to another argument and her dismissal. And now that she had another chance to stay at Wallaroo, she wasn't about to cut the ground from under her own feet.

She took a deep breath and looked at him directly. 'No. Your cousin Lucette hired me in Melbourne. We travelled up here together.'

'Really?' He allowed his sapphire gaze to linger on her approvingly. She could feel beads of perspiration forming on her skin as if the sun was reaching right into her room. 'My little cousin shows great taste. I hope I've thanked her appropriately.'

Ally almost choked, remembering how before the accident, he had jeered, *She couldn't have found anyone less suitable than you!*

She drew in a sharp breath, then bit down quickly on her lip. 'You probably didn't have time,' she muttered, hoping against hope that Ned had kept his word and provided a plausible explanation for how Fletcher came to be crossing the Fanning River with her so quickly after she arrived.

Easing his wide shoulder away from the doorframe, he

took a step into her room and Ally almost jumped out of her skin. If she just reached out she could touch his brown forearm. Another step and she would be able to smell his familiar, tangy aftershave and the subtle, muskiness of his skin.

The cat stood up in the middle of the bed, stretched and miaowed, then jumped down and padded towards Fletcher to rub his golden head against his master's legs. If only I belonged here like you do, Lightbulb, Ally thought.

'I hear you've taken on quite a few chores, perhaps more than necessary,' Fletcher commented.

Shrugging, Ally spread her damp palms down her thighs to dry them. He seemed intrigued by the movement and she quickly closed her fists.

'I like to keep busy,' she said quietly.

'And you like purple,' he responded with yet another sizzling smile while her mind whirled crazily and her body froze.

'How do you know? How could you possibly know about that unless...'

'Unless?'

Unless he remembered intimate details of their relationship! She had to clutch the carved post at the end of the bed for support as she remembered Fletcher smiling at her shyly from behind an enormous bunch of orchids.

Fletcher let his gaze rest on her for a thoughtful moment and her nerve endings jangled. His eyes gleamed with gentle mockery as he observed the confusion in her blushing cheeks and her obvious need for support.

'I'm sorry if I've embarrassed you, Miss Fraser,' he murmured, turning her skin to goose bumps of apprehension.

She tried to pretend nonchalance. 'Not at all. I was just surprised that...that you...' It didn't work. She couldn't

talk her way out of this one. The lazy amusement in his
eyes sparked her anger and she retaliated without thinking. 'Well, how did you know?'

'That you have a fetish for purple underwear?'

'It's hardly a fetish...a fondness perhaps... But?'

She couldn't continue. It felt distinctly absurd to be
discussing such intimate details with a man she hardly
knew and yet, at the same time, knew as closely and
completely as she knew herself. It was desperately confusing. She felt ill.

Then she caught his amused gaze. He was almost
winking at her before switching his gaze to the piles of
clothes on her bed. She looked and blushed again. There,
next to neat piles of T-shirts, socks and undies for
Connor, were piles of her clothes. A couple of blouses
were set aside waiting to be ironed, but next to them were
her bras—white lace, coffee satin, wispy and dainty and
then a pile of her panties. They were clearly on display—
purple stripes, purple hearts, purple spots and flowers,
lilac lace and violet satin—some of which Fletcher himself had purchased.

His comment had been based entirely on his observa-
tion of her folded washing and it didn't take a Sherlock
Holmes to come to the same conclusion he had.

Such clear evidence of his loss of memory brought a
huge wave of cold sadness, as if an ocean of Antarctic
water had been dumped on her.

She swept her eyes up to his and tried to shrug casually.

'You've caught me out already, Mr. Hardy.'

'I guess I shouldn't come barging into a young lady's
boudoir,' he replied gallantly. He gestured towards the
doorway. 'Come and take a little walk with me. I need
to have a bit of a look at the old place. I feel as if I've
been away six months instead of just a week.' Then he

frowned and once more grinned endearingly. This time, though, the smile was a little lopsided. 'I guess in one sense I have been away that long.' His hand ran swiftly across his brow and took a deep breath.

The amnesia bothered him, but he was pretending it wasn't a problem, Ally decided. For a brief moment, he looked lost, all alone. As if he needed someone. If only she could offer him some comfort—even a little squeeze of the hand.

'You should have seen this place from the air—water everywhere—just what this country needed,' he said, shooting her a swift glance as if warning her that he wanted no sympathy.

She hunted around for something practical to discuss and suddenly remembered, with a surge of guilt, her responsibilities.

'Should I collect Connor? He must have finished his afternoon tea by now,' she offered hurriedly.

'He's onto seconds.' He took her arm to guide her out of the room and Ally almost flinched at his touch. 'Let Mary spoil him,' he said with a chuckle. 'She looked after me when I was a nipper and I loved it. Now, enough of these formalities. Can we get straight to first names, Alexandra?'

The terrible tension which had seized her as soon as he arrived tightened another notch. She struggled to make her voice sound normal.

'Oh, please, call me Ally. Everybody does. I only use Alexandra for...' Gulping, sucking in a quick breath, she thanked her lucky stars that she'd stopped herself in time. She'd been about to mention her career, but a sixth sense warned her to avoid talking about fashion to this new Fletcher. 'I mean, Alexandra sounds so formal, doesn't it?'

'Not as bad as Mr. Hardy. I won't hear that again, will I, Ally?'

She shook her head slowly, unable to speak. The pleasant camaraderie he was so quickly establishing caught her completely off guard. It was so very different from the afternoon she had arrived. And it was nothing at all like the evening they first met. His fascination with her then had left him quite tongue-tied. There was none of that tension now.

Fletcher led her to a timber garden seat under one of the huge tamarind trees flanking the front lawn. From there they had a view of the whole of the front of the homestead. Ally sat rather primly beside him, fearfully conscious of his relaxed sprawl. His long legs stretched interminably in front of him, while a casual arm rested lightly along the back of the seat. He showed absolutely none of her unease. There was definitely no sign that he was experiencing any of the vibrating physical awareness that was causing her such discomfort.

'Ah, it's good to be home and such a pleasant surprise to find the company has expanded so delightfully,' he said with another of his heart-stopping grins.

Wallaroo Downs, the home that Fletcher had so clearly missed, had what real estate agents might have termed 'street appeal' if it had been anywhere near a city. It was a long, low house set back behind a wide expanse of lawn. One end of the long, deep front veranda was enclosed with lattice over which sprawled a rioting cascade of crimson bougainvillea.

Enormous tubs of tropical palms and hanging baskets of ferns were dotted along the veranda. And, in gardens stretching on either side of the front steps, were masses of vividly coloured shrubs—poinsettia, hibiscus, crotons and acalyphas kept alive through the drought by Ned who'd linked up an ingenious irrigation system from the creek. The reds, pinks and oranges of these shrubs provided a lively contrast to the deep shady trees whose trunks were home to enormous staghorns and bush orchids and beneath which sheltered more ferns. Already, in a week, Ally had become very fond of the house and garden.

Mary, bearing a large wicker tray, ambled towards them, her round cheery face flushed and beaming.

'Ah, Mary. Thanks so much.' Fletcher sprang to his feet and helped the housekeeper to settle the tray onto the low garden table beside where they sat.

Ally knew she looked surprised. 'Mary, how lovely.'

The tray held afternoon tea things—a coffeepot, two mugs, a milk jug and sugar basin—all made of beautiful earthenware pottery. There was also a plate of Mary's delicious pumpkin scones with little tubs of butter, jam and cream. Ally felt embarrassed. She was, after all, only supposed to be the hired help and now here she was being treated more like a special guest. Mary gave her a shy grin and quickly made to depart.

'How's Connor behaving?' Ally felt compelled to call after her.

'Like a little lamb,' Mary reassured her almost too heartily and as quickly as her bulky shape would allow, she scuttled away across the lawn and into the house.

'How do you like your coffee?' Fletcher asked, as if he noticed nothing at all strange about Mary's manner. He lifted the pot and the aroma drifted towards her. 'They don't make coffee like this in the hospital,' he said with an appreciative sniff.

'Oh, white, no sugar,' she responded automatically.

Fletcher handed her a cup of coffee and poured one for himself. Ally took a sip. It was very strong, brewed coffee—perhaps what she needed to give her stamina to face this strange situation. His eyes, as he looked at her over the rim of his coffee mug, had taken on a smoky haze that softened their brightness and she wondered, just for a moment, if perhaps he wasn't quite as confident and relaxed as he pretended.

But his next question showed her that she couldn't afford to let her mind wander. She needed to be as alert as a witness before a Royal Commission.

'Tell me about yourself,' he drawled softly. 'What experience have you had of life on a cattle property?'

The huge gulp of coffee scalded her throat and, while she desperately didn't want to cough and splutter, that was exactly what she did. Loudly and dramatically. She couldn't have reacted more guiltily if she had suddenly donned dark glasses and a raincoat. Her behaviour didn't go unnoticed.

Fletcher's eyes cooled and narrowed and he straightened to a more erect, alert seating position. 'Do you need water?' he asked politely, guardedly.

'No, no. I'm sorry. The coffee was hotter than I realised,' she stammered. She quickly replaced the coffee cup on its saucer and reached for a scone. Without butter or jam she bit into it, her mind racing, her heart hammering and her throat so tight she wondered how she would ever be able to swallow the small morsel.

And even more importantly, how on earth was she ever going to answer this question? In just thirty seconds she could tell this man enough to have him reject her out of hand. The truth would have him standing and towering over her, his beautiful mouth grim and disdaining, as he informed her that unfortunately there'd been a misunderstanding and she was not suitable for the position of nanny on Wallaroo Downs. Once again she would be packing her bags and being dismissed. A dreadful sense of futility and failure threatened to swamp her so completely that she almost sobbed.

But Ally had never given in. The tough dog-eat-dog world of high fashion had presented her with many knocks, scores of seemingly impossible challenges, and always, she'd hung in there, keeping her goal in sight. This, she decided quickly, was just one more challenge. This time her goal was even more important. Fletcher Hardy meant more to her than fashion design ever had.

'I…I grew up in…' she began. To her horror she heard her voice sounding uncertain…timorous. This wasn't good enough. She needed to lift her act.

Fletcher leaned forward, his attention fixed on her with total concentration. She sat beside him, rigid with fear, willing herself to continue. Her racing heart would not calm down and her breathing was out of control. In the trees behind her a flock of apostle birds began their noisy squabbling. Think of what it will mean if you have to go back to Melbourne, she told herself. Think of never see-ing him again!

Summoning every ounce of strength she possessed, she lifted her head and looked straight into his beautiful blue eyes.

'I grew up on a cattle property down near Rockhampton,' she lied in a cool, controlled voice. 'Friendship Creek station. You've heard of it?' she added with just the right shade of curiosity, knowing that he couldn't have. The name had popped into her head as she spoke.

His eyes narrowed and he gazed at her thoughtfully, his glance running over her, sending quivers darting down her back.

'No, I haven't,' he remarked, breaking his gaze to take one of Mary's scones and spread it liberally with home-made Burdekin plum jam.

'It's not far from Mt. Freedom station,' she supplied,

quickly throwing in the name of the place where she had spent several school holidays.

'Ah, yes. I know that place. Quite a big property. Belongs to the Savages.'

'Yes, that's right.' She took a quick breath to help gather her composure.

He smiled at her again and as usual the charm worked. She felt warm, glowing relief seep into her veins. It seemed her deception, terrible as it was, would be worth it.

She should have known his charming smile was the result of a lucky mix of genes and was not an indication of a sensitive, courteous nature. It was in fact as dangerous as a crocodile's leer.

'Tell me,' he said, 'how Lucette came to choose you to be Connor's nanny.'

For an awful moment, all she could think of was the truth. How she had begged Lucette to allow her to come. How she had plotted and schemed to arrive at Wallaroo Downs with Connor and win back Fletcher's heart. How futile that scheme had proved was so strongly impressed on her now, that for the life of her she could not think past it.

'Lucette knew that when I was at Art College I'd been a nanny for the children of two doctors in Melbourne.'

Fletcher inclined his head. 'Art College?' He leaned back in the seat. 'Tell me what else you do.'

Hesitantly, she began, treading cautiously around the truth, using just enough to give her story substance. 'I've tried to make a living from art. I always wanted to be a fashion designer…but it's so hard to get into that field. So I've drifted a bit…I've done a little modelling, some freelance sketching for calendars and…and some work as a nanny.' It was amazing really, how once she started to lie, the rest came so easily. As she spoke, he watched her. He watched the way she talked and the movement of her hands as she developed her story.

He was watching so closely that she wondered if he could see through her artifice. Her skin was so very fair. She didn't really look like she'd spent much time out in the bush. Her hands were soft and white and carefully manicured, each finger tipped by a well-shaped nail and revealing a neat half moon; not like Mary's which were rough and red from years of hard housework, or Fletcher's, which were brown and callused. Her deception weighed on her like a heavy yoke.

She had fought hard for what she wanted before, but she'd always fought fairly. But now the stakes were higher. If she could somehow win Fletcher back, surely a few little lies would be worth it.

He didn't comment. His deeply blue eyes squinted thoughtfully as though he were trying to will his memory to return so that he could match up her story with what he already knew. What he used to know.

She drank the rest of her coffee hardly tasting it. If she blew her chances now, there would be no more. She looked at him steadily, trying to hide the yearning from her face. If she wanted to prove her usefulness on a cattle property, she would have to concentrate on practicalities and forget romance completely.

Forget it as completely as Fletcher had.

She was distracted from her thoughts by Fletcher leaning forward to replace his coffee cup on the wicker tray. He sent another of his caressing smiles rippling over Ally before he spoke. 'As I said before, it's great to have you as part of our little team. Lucette has shown admirable judgment. Now I guess I'd better let you get back to your young charge.'

He stood up, towering above her and then bent towards

her with the relaxed, unconscious confidence of well-bred manners, a hand at her elbow.

'I'd like to see Connor really experience a taste of life here. Let him play with the dogs. I have the perfect pony in mind for him, so you can teach him to ride. Take him fishing when the waters go down—that sort of thing... You do know how to fish, don't you?'

'Um...yes. I know the basics.' She knew that you needed a hook on the end of a line.

'And of course, you know the most important thing to teach him.'

Her grey eyes widened. 'I do?'

His serious expression made her suddenly nervous. 'To have absolute respect for his godfather.'

She almost punched him for that and she couldn't resist putting him in his place. 'Absolute respect cannot be demanded,' she replied archly. 'It must be earned. Connor's godfather has a responsibility to provide an impeccable role model.'

His blue eyes gleamed like expensively cut sapphires. 'Not a problem.'

Then as if in retaliation to her impudence, his hand moved towards her and she felt it brush her neck and sweep back a wing of hair from her face. The fleeting touch made her tremble helplessly and every instinct urged her to lean into the curve of his hand, but somehow Ally willed herself to pull away.

'Except that—I'll also be—' he murmured, as his fingers traced a path up the violet ribbon that tied back her hair.

'What are you doing?' she gasped.

Fletcher did not answer. He simply stood there, his warm hand against her cheek, his deep forget-me-not eyes studying her thoughtfully. Ally's heart began to jog and then to canter erratically.

'I'm remembering...' he said eventually.

'Re-remembering? Really?' She blanched, faint with alarm. If his memory had returned already, that heart-wrenching smile was about to turn to disgust as the full truth dawned on him.

'Yes,' he went on huskily. 'I'm remembering all those lovely purple garments of yours. If you want me to behave impeccably, don't leave anything like them lying around, Ally.'

Then, he smiled down at her slowly, seductively, so that she wanted to curl herself into his arms. She felt her lips part and her entire body fill with an overwhelming yearning for the warmth of his body against hers once more, to run her fingers through his thick glossy hair, to have his mouth hungrily devouring hers. The force of her feelings terrified her. At any minute she would give herself away.

But, totally unaware of her turmoil, Fletcher turned casually and strode off across the lawn and back towards the homestead.

CHAPTER SEVEN

ALLY managed to get through the next few days without a mishap and by the end of the week was beginning to feel more relaxed. For most of the day, Fletcher was gone, taking off to different parts of the property, and at night they dined with Ned, Mary and Connor.

She was grateful to be able to keep well out of Fletcher's way. Any time alone with him could spell disaster. What she needed was enough time before he regained his memory to prove to him that here on this property with him was where she belonged.

And she also needed to comply with some of his requests. There was no way she could teach a four-year-old boy to ride Fletcher's 'perfect pony,' so she decided to settle on fishing.

The floodwaters had almost completely receded and the creek below Wallaroo homestead, although a little more swollen than before the rain, was flowing once more at a sedate, leisurely pace. The muddiness had given way to fresh, clear water that sparkled in the afternoon sunlight.

It was quite fun to spend a lazy afternoon supervising Connor's first attempts with a fishing line. The grass on the creek bank had already sprung back fresh and lush after the recent rain, and the sun had dried and warmed it so that she found it was a perfect spot to sprawl in old denim shorts and a T-shirt.

Smiling to herself as she watched Connor staring eagerly into the water below, she realised that she wasn't really missing her work at all. She looked around at the gently whispering bush and at the distant hills warm and golden in the westerly sun and released a happy, satisfied sigh.

It was so beautiful here, so peaceful. A picture of Melbourne with hooting traffic and jammed streets, the smell of petrol fumes and jostling, busy, people-filled shopping malls flitted across her mind. For most of her life, she had enjoyed being a part of the rat race. Until now, she'd always lived in a metropolitan city, and she found the frenetic pace invigorating, but looking at the picture postcard scene before her, she wondered if she could ever enjoy it quite so much again.

Here, the air was clear and still and the corellas and budgerigars provided a delightful background chorus. If it weren't for the constant fear of her lies being revealed, she could certainly feel at peace. I could so easily be happy here, she thought. Why can't Fletcher understand that?

'Why won't the fishy bite my hook?' Connor asked Ally for the umpteenth time, as he plonked his muddy self at her feet. Ally shook her head in frustration. She had no idea and she was beginning to share the little boy's weariness with the sport of fishing. At least for her, there was an afternoon's enjoyment of the quiet, chuckling stream and the tranquil bush to delight in, but such pleasures were unlikely to impress a four-year-old.

'Would you like to stop fishing and make some boats?' she asked.

'Stop fishing? That's no way to teach him patience,' a familiar, masculine voice erupted behind them. Fletcher loomed above, walking his horse along the top of the bank.

Ally winced. His approach must have been silenced by

the leafy bush track. If Fletcher was about to inspect her methods of teaching the noble art of fishing, she was in deep trouble. And as he dismounted and tethered his stallion to a nearby tree, she realised that was exactly what he had in mind.

'Any luck, mate?' he asked Connor in the man-to-man tone he had come to adopt with his godson and which the boy clearly relished. Connor looked up at his hero as he strode down the creek bank, his eyes shining with respect, but then he looked at Ally and pulled a face.

'No, fishing's boring.'

'Good grief, Ally.' Fletcher pointed to Connor's fishing rod then turned to her with a mixture of puzzlement and fury. 'What do you call that?'

'He's only a little boy playing at fishing,' she muttered defensively, then added, 'It's his fishing rod, of course,'

'It's a bloody log!'

She ducked her head. 'Well I made it from a tree branch. I thought it had to be reasonably thick so it wouldn't break when the fish pulled on the line.'

Fletcher stepped toward Connor and held out his hand for the boy to surrender his fishing tackle, shaking his head in amazement as he examined Ally's fearful construction. 'A tree branch, red string, a huge safety pin and no bait, Ally? What in hell's name were you expecting the boy to catch with that? A bunyip?'

'What's a bunyip?' asked Connor, but for once Fletcher ignored him. He was waiting for Ally's answer, his expression tyrannical.

'There *was* bait. I put a worm on. I've a whole bucketful of worms.' She'd dug the disgusting things up herself and been very proud of her willingness to get her hands so filthy.

'Good. Show me how you baited the hook.'

'Fine,' Ally replied with an air of hurt dignity, not liking at all the tone of his voice. 'I just pick one up, like this.' She tried particularly hard not to pull a face as she extracted a worm from the muddy bucket, and did her best to hold the squirming, slippery invertebrate casually, but firmly. 'And I stick it on the hook like this.'

'Is that all?'

'What do you mean, is that all? What else is there to do?'

'For Pete's sake, Ally, there's no way that worm will stay on that hook. You've simply jabbed it through once. It would probably slip off the minute it hits the water. You have to thread a hook—and I mean a proper hook, not this poor excuse for one—through the worm several times to make it stay on.'

'Not always,' she replied airily. His lecturing tone was irritating enough to make her defiantly toss the baited safety pin back into the water.

'There's no way you'll catch a fish with that. And just for the record, what's with the red string?' Fletcher shoved his thumbs into his belt loops and favoured Ally with a disparaging sneer.

'It's the only sort I had. I brought it with me for Connor. Children like bright colours and…well…I thought maybe it wouldn't matter. Didn't you know fish are colour blind?'

The blue eyes bored into hers. 'If that's the case,' he drawled, 'why is it, do you think, that fishermen go to so much expense to buy clear, monofilament lines?'

She stared at him, furious, wishing some clever answer could spring to her lips, but no words would come. Instead she felt like slapping that beautiful, smug face. She was trying, damn him. She was trying so hard to be a good nanny. Since when did nannies have to be experts on all aspects of male sports? Next he would probably want Connor taught Rugby and cricket. Connor had no complaints. Why couldn't Fletcher just leave her to get on with her job?

The branch nearly jumped out of her hand.

'What was that?' she asked, and immediately blushed at her foolishness. There was no doubt what it was.

'I think you have a bite,' offered Fletcher dryly.

Ally held the shaking branch with both hands as she felt the powerful tug on the line. 'W-what do I do?'

A dark eyebrow rose questioningly. 'My dear Ally, it's quite simple. You pull it in.' He was mocking her, looking down with sardonic amusement at her dilemma. How could he do this to her?

But what he did next was worse.

Two strong arms came round her to take the rod and she felt Fletcher's breath fan the nape of her neck as he tugged at the string. Against her back she could feel the muscled breadth of his chest and his denim-clad thighs hard against her buttocks. She knew she shouldn't allow his entire body to mould so firmly against hers, but her own body ignored any feeble warnings her mind tried to transmit as the warmth of him, mingled with his heated, manly smell, enveloped her.

The fish came out of the water with a splash, gleaming silver, thrashing and struggling on the line. Somewhere nearby she could hear Connor's excited squeals. If she could have spoken, she would have begged Fletcher to return the fish to the creek, to leave it to swim free. But the closeness of him, the delicious pressure of his body against hers, robbed her of any hope of speech. She didn't take much notice of how he landed the fish, but she was very, very aware of the startling location of Fletcher's mouth.

It would only take the slightest sideways movement of her head to have her lips touching his. A surge of heat scorched through Ally's body. I should be backing off from this, one part of her brain urged her. But then as strong fingers gently lifted her chin, coaxing her round, tempting her to lean even more deeply into him, she remained silent.

Why was she allowing this to happen? she asked herself dazedly, as she recognized the fierce darkening of desire in his eyes. Surely this wasn't wise? She ought to struggle—to protest—push him away. If Fletcher knew her real identity, he would not be breathing so raggedly. His hands would not be sliding so sensuously down her back, sending shivers of pleasure rippling through her entire body. She shouldn't just stand there, quivering with desire, her tongue tip flickering over her lips, willing this man who didn't know her to take her mouth with his.

Which was exactly what he did.

She thought she knew all the secrets of Fletcher's lovemaking, but she was unprepared for the seductive gentleness of his kiss. It was as if he were drinking a delicate wine, tasting her slowly, exploring her mouth with mesmerising thoroughness and extracting from her the most flaring, uncontrolled desire. His heartbeat was pounding close to hers. She wanted to moan, to sink down onto the grassy bank and have that mouth continue its sensuous journey. Even though he did not know it, this was her man...her lover and she wanted his kisses to go on forever.

But he was drawing away, his blue eyes regretful, his hands still resting possessively on her slim hips. Then he looked down and she followed his gaze. Connor was standing tugging at the knees of Fletcher's jeans.

'Uncle Fletcher, Uncle Fletcher, what's a bunyip?'

Fletcher released her, smiling a long, slow sigh, which ended in a rueful chuckle. He allowed his eyes, sultry with desire to linger on Ally.

Her mouth was dry. Every nerve, every pulse in her body wanted him to continue what he had begun. If Connor had not been there, she knew she would have disgraced herself. She would have dragged Fletcher down onto the bank and torn off her clothes, begging him to take her eager breasts into that gorgeous mouth of his.

Her mind was filled with memories of Fletcher's beautiful body—all muscle and taut, sun-drenched skin, needing her, loving her, taking her.

His soft voice stirred her back to the present. 'I must apologise.'

She drew in a sharp breath at the unexpectedness of his words. The Fletcher she knew would certainly never have apologised for stealing a kiss. Trying unsuccessfully not to appear surprised, Ally stuttered, 'Yes, Mr.—um, Fletcher, that—that was uncalled for.'

Once more, a strong finger was beneath Ally's chin, tilting back her head so that she was forced to look up into his narrowed eyes. 'Nothing uncalled for has happened, Ally. Now, before you get those lovely purple knickers in a knot, I am not apologising for tasting your sweet mouth, little nanny…it's my criticism of your fishing line that was wrong. Obviously it's just what silver perch like,' he added with a sparkling grin.

Then, while she disintegrated into a jigsaw puzzle of conflicting emotions, wanting to simultaneously hug him and thump him, Fletcher calmly reached down and lifted a delighted Connor onto his shoulders as easily as if he were a silk necktie.

'How'd you like a ride on my horse, youngster?'

'Oh, yes please,' breathed Connor, his eyes round and shining.

'And,' added Fletcher as he placed the perch in a canvas bag hanging from a saddle strap, 'thanks to Ally, you can have fresh, fried fish for your dinner.'

'Yum! Can I have chips, too?'

'We'll have to talk to Mary about that. Now say goodbye to Ally.' The blue eyes flickered gently over her.

'Does Ally have to walk all by herself?'

'Oh, Connor, it's only across the paddock, you know that,' Ally said quickly.

Then she watched Fletcher lift Connor high up onto the big, black steed. She frowned as she noticed a moment of fear pucker his little face when he found himself alone on the stallion's back. But he was all smiles again as soon as Fletcher was mounted behind him.

'But tell me really and truly, what is a bunyip?' she heard the little boy's piping voice ask again as the horse set off and she watched them go, man and boy, the makings of a new family, while the alarming sensations aroused by his kiss remained surging through her.

Alone on the creek bank, Ally didn't move to follow them. She was lost in her memories of the taste of Fletcher, his smell, the feel of him, and of her own clamouring senses yearning for him. Wrapping her arms around herself, she frowned, feeling quite miserable again. She couldn't afford to let something like that kiss happen again, but did she have the strength to prevent it? And where could her venture to Wallaroo Downs possibly be heading, except headlong into disaster?

If Fletcher became interested in her for a second time and then found out again who she really was, he would be doubly furious with her. He would hate her for deceiving him.

There was no doubt she was taking a foolish risk in staying on Fletcher's property under false pretences when there was almost no chance it could turn out well.

But there was no way she could bring herself to leave. Everything would be so much easier if she could. She almost wished that she didn't have to love him, but that was as impossible as changing the weather; it was something she couldn't alter or escape from. She was more certain of that now than ever before, but, given Fletcher's attitude to Alexandra Fraser, fashion designer, her feelings about him were never going to be satisfied.

She sighed heavily. Everything had seemed so easy before she set out for North Queensland. She was so sure that all she had to do was show Fletcher how happy she was to live in the bush and take care of Connor and he would ask her to marry him. But Fletcher the master of Wallaroo Downs obviously had a different set of priorities from the happy lover of Melbourne.

The day was turning to dusk, time to go back. Ally shrugged herself out of her mist of thoughts and climbed to the top of the bank. From the creek, frogs croaked, and Ally could hear cicadas humming in the trees. The sky over the hills was flushed with the blushing, late afternoon colour of ripened mangoes and already the evening star was blinking.

The transition from dusk to night was short and swift in the tropics.

By the time she returned from the creek bank, she found Connor eagerly watching Mary preparing his fish for supper. He seemed fascinated by the shiny, sharp knife as it sliced the fillets from the backbone.

I guess that's another extremely useful skill that a good bush woman has, Ally thought with a grumpy sigh.

Mary looked across at her, her eyes shrewd, but sparkling as if they were lit by an inner excitement. 'So to-night's the big night. A proper dinner party for you and Fletcher—how lovely.'

'Really?' Ally asked, not sure how she felt about this news.

'Good idea,' chipped in Ned who had just come in from setting sprinklers around the homestead garden.

'I'd consider it a privilege to put the little fella to bed if he's still awake,' added Mary.

Why does this feel like a conspiracy? Ally asked herself as she looked at the grinning couple. Ned seated himself at one end of the roomy kitchen table and began to chop vegetables for Mary, who was looking remarkably satisfied with the state of affairs. Mary was giving the fish scraps to an ecstatic Lightbulb and Connor was watching with fascination. Then all three looked at Ally expectantly.

'I haven't been consulted about any dinner party,' she said stiffly, finding their curiosity stifling.

'Well, that's as may be,' mused Mary. 'But I've got my orders.'

'And Fletcher needs a little partyin',' added Ned. 'And so do you, lass. Young people need to—to—enjoy themselves a bit.'

Ally resisted telling them both that under the circumstances, parties—in this case, the dinner for two that Fletcher had obviously conned them into—would not bring enjoyment to either herself or to Fletcher. It would almost certainly end in her revealing something about her past that would incriminate her. It would be as dangerous as whitewater rafting without a paddle.

But if the dinner was risky, it was also beautiful. Mary's cooking was a surprise. The wholesome meals she had served until now had led Ally to assume that on a cattle property, one always ate beef—as steak, or roast, corned or casseroled. But tonight they dined on delicious seafood garnered from the huge cold room at the back of the kitchen. It was dressed in a delicate, creamy sauce and accompanied by fettuccini and a crisp garden salad. The table was set with antique silver on an immaculate, starched, white damask cloth.

And, what was even more pleasing, was that, rather than attacking her with personal questions, Fletcher seemed happy enough with the relatively harmless topics Ally neatly introduced herself—initially questions about Connor's parents and then about the families who lived on the surrounding properties.

She found herself beginning to relax a little—perhaps with the help of the classic, dry white wine, which she was drinking a little too quickly. As long as the conversation stayed general and kept well away from the personal, she was safe, she reassured herself. So she was caught out by the unexpected.

'You look beautiful this evening, Ally.'

Twin reactions of pleasure and alarm swamped her suddenly. She had dressed carefully in a simple but elegantly cut linen dress and had blown her hair dry to sit neatly just above her shoulders. She thought she had managed to look neat and ordinary, just as a nanny should.

'I can see why you wear that colour—the colour of violets. It makes your eyes go all smoky and mauve like distant hills at sunset.'

Fletcher waxing poetical! It was enough to make her put down her crystal wineglass very smartly and think seriously about eating. Even more than revealing her true identity, she was desperately afraid of letting down her guard and revealing her true feelings. If she wanted to stay on Wallaroo Downs, it was imperative that she continued to appear indifferent to Fletcher Hardy's charm—especially after the afternoon's little lapse.

Ally mumbled her acknowledgment of his praise and swiftly steered the conversation back to books and travel—subjects she knew were safe from their discussions in Melbourne. The candlelight, the good food and more of the beautiful Clare Valley Chardonnay combined with the formidable charm of Fletcher's company; all worked their magic so that she was lulled once more into a sensuous, relaxed mood. A surge of sheer, unalloyed desire streamed through her veins. Heavens above, she thought, lowering long lashes over her telltale eyes, how can I ever pretend I'm not madly in love with this man?

Their romance had started at the wrong end, of course—mad, passionate lovemaking, with only sketchy understandings of each other as a person. Now, the more she learned about Fletcher, the more certain she was that she was in the right place with the right man.

'I think you should come on a tour of the property with me.' Fletcher's words startled her out of her musings. 'I want to check out some of the outer areas before we start the muster—I can't for the life of me remember where all my cattle are,' he continued. 'And you can get to know a bit more about the place. Mary will mind the little chap for a day or two. She'd love it.'

He looked across at her, his blue eyes twinkling and his smile warm and charming.

'Would—would we be riding horses?' Ally asked cautiously, not allowing herself to think about how those blue eyes would chill and the smile vanish if he knew that at best she could only ride at a slow canter.

Fletcher's smile glowed in the subdued lighting. 'We'll do it in style and throw our swags and an esky in the back of the Range Rover.' His eyes slid over her slim frame. 'I figure that neat little behind of yours would be black, blue and purple after a day in the saddle.'

'Well, you're right,' Ally admitted carefully. 'It has been a while since I left the bush.'

'So you'd like to come with me?'

'Yes, I'd love to.' The eager words had left her lips before she considered just how enthusiastic they sounded. Too late, she realised that she had just volunteered for more time alone with Fletcher, more opportunities to stir his memory. She looked away quickly, but not before she caught a curious sparkle in Fletcher's eyes.

'Good, that's settled then,' he said quietly.

After breakfast the next day, Connor, with Mary at his side, waved them off from the front veranda quite happily. They left with the morning sky still streaked with pink and gold. Ally sat quietly, remembering the last time she had driven beside Fletcher when he'd been escorting her off his station. Now he was taking her on the grand tour and she should have been relaxed and thrilled that he wanted to share his home with her.

If only she didn't have to feel so guilty.

What bothered her was the knowledge that as each day passed, the moment when his memory returned drew nearer. Over and over again, Ally tried to convince herself that she wasn't being foolish. Given a little more time, surely she could convince him that her place was beside him here at Wallaroo Downs.

She thought of the two swags, rolled and buckled and lying side by side in the back of the vehicle. Tonight, she and Fletcher would no doubt be lying side by side. They would be camping under the stars, sleeping together in the bush. A heated coil of pleasure uncurled deep inside her. Did he plan to continue where the other day's kiss left off?

Would she make love to him, knowing that she was deceiving him?

Could she resist?

There were kilometres of plains, no longer dry and dusty but lush with bright, fresh grass stretching around them on all sides.

'Best sight a cattleman could ever hope to see,' said Fletcher nodding at the vast stretches of grassland.

As they bumped along the dirt track, Ally found herself drinking in the wide expanse—blue sky going on forever and the grey-green plains dotted with cattle and reaching to the distant, purple hills.

'That's where we're going to camp tonight,' Fletcher said, nodding his head towards the hills, 'on the river bank at the foot of that range.'

Ally concentrated on the scenery close by, unwilling to let her mind dwell any further on the night to come. But her eyes were continually drawn back to the man beside her. Silhouetted against the bright sunlight outside the Range Rover's cabin, every detail of the man she loved was clearly defined. The little bump on the bridge of his nose, the unexpected symmetry of his mouth, the dark curls emerging from his open collar, and the power in his hands as they rested lightly on the steering wheel. He had looked wonderful in the city, but here in the bush where he belonged, with the wide, vast outback all around, he looked perfect.

They stopped for lunch on the edge of the Burdekin River. Enormous paperbarks curtained the banks, some still standing in water, a legacy of the recent rains. And as Ally and Fletcher munched on their sandwiches and downed cans of cold beer from the esky, he pointed out black ducks, pelicans, wood ducks and egrets flitting across the water, or swooping to catch fish. Behind them, huge basalt outcrops loomed majestically like castles on the Rhine.

Ally was overawed by the sheer drama of the setting with the wide river full of busy bird life, the imposing trees with their beautiful trunks of creamy, peeling bark and the towering cliffs of grey stone. Everything was bathed in clear, bright sunlight beneath a brilliant blue sky.

'Wallaroo Downs is a beautiful property,' she said. 'It must mean a lot to you.'

Fletcher stretched back and rested on his elbow. 'This spot always blows me away. Of course, everything always looks better after some rain. It's not always this pretty.'

'Oh, I know. I did arrive here before the rain, remember?'

'No, I don't,' Fletcher replied quietly, and Ally bit down hard on her lip. She saw a shadow of annoyance cross his features and he picked up a small stone and threw it fiercely into the river, causing some ducks to take off with loud, protesting honks. He looked away, down the river and then to the rocks behind them. 'Want to climb up there?' he asked, as if to change the subject.

'Sure,' she responded.

Ally was glad she had worn sturdy boots as she clambered up the rocks behind Fletcher. As they reached the top, a fresh breeze drifted up from the river.

'This is just amazing,' murmured Ally, looking with total awe at the wall of rock beneath her, the wide Burdekin River below and the rolling green country stretching away on the far side.

'It's pretty amazing to think it was all under the sea

once,' Fletcher said, crouching on the blue-grey rock and tracing its surface with his hand.

'You're kidding?'

'Not at all. Look at this.' Fletcher reached up and took her hand, pulling her down beside him. He was pointing at a mark in the rocks. Ally looked more closely.

'It looks like a—a piece of coral,' she said.

'That's right,' he said. 'It's fossilised coral. And that's a mollusc and there's more coral over there. And what do you think this little curly thing could be?'

'Oh, I don't know. It's a kind of horn or something.'

'It's a form of ammonite. A little sea creature from the Mesozoic Era. They became extinct around the same time as the dinosaurs.'

'Really?' breathed Ally.

'Millions of years ago, before the ice age, this was all under the sea. Hard to believe, isn't it?'

'Thinking about the land and how long it's been around—it always makes our little lives seem rather insignificant, doesn't it?'

'Oh, I don't know,' mused Fletcher. 'Perhaps if we take ourselves too seriously it might. I rather like to think of myself as a part of it all. I want my bones to rest here one day—become part of the land again.'

'You really love this country, don't you?' Ally asked softly.

'It's in my blood.'

Ally felt her breath catch as he turned to look to the south so that his profile beneath its shady hat was silhouetted clearly against the bright sky.

I love it, too, she wanted to say, but she contented herself with, 'It's going to be a wonderful place for Connor to grow up.'

Fletcher grinned, then stood up beside her. 'Always

the little nanny,' he chuckled. 'Come on, let's go or we won't make the hills before dark.'

Ally spent the afternoon relishing the cosy, companionable peace. Fletcher rattled the four-wheel-drive vehicle along the bumpy track, at times stopping to check on stock or on the condition of fences, or to show Ally a particularly interesting landmark. As the shadows lengthened, tawny kangaroos emerged from the bush to join the grazing cattle while overhead, squadrons of flying foxes winged silently across the reddening sky to feed on ti-tree blossoms. Ally felt so happy and peaceful. Everything would have been just perfect if she could have curled up on the seat beside Fletcher and rested her head on his broad shoulder.

The track wound back down to the river bank again. At the point where they set up camp, the grassy bank was high on their side and low and sandy on the far side of the river. Together they gathered some firewood and piled it at a perfect spot for a campfire where they would have a view up and down the river.

'Time for a swim,' said Fletcher, and immediately began to pull off his shirt. As the broad, brown back emerged, rippling and male in the red-gold light of dusk, Ally nervously wondered if he would be swimming naked.

'What—what about crocodiles?'

Fletcher shot her a reassuring smile. 'Not this far inland. There might be the odd freshwater croc, but they only eat fish.'

'Well—I brought my bathers,' she said quickly, disappearing behind the truck to change. By the time she re-emerged, wearing a demure black one-piece swimsuit, Fletcher was already in the water. He turned over, floating on his back and watching her as she self-consciously made her way down the steep bank. She knew he was having a long look at her slim figure and legs. To her own surprise, she found herself posing on a log at the water's edge. Have an eyeful, Fletch, she told him silently. You found me pretty irresistible once.

Then she slipped into the cool water and boldly swam towards him.

Fletcher remained, treading water, watching her as she drew nearer. Ally switched to breaststroke so that she could observe his face as she swam slowly up to him. His eyes were fixed intently on her.

A few metres away, her heart began to thump painfully in her chest. I'm going to seduce him, she realised. It hadn't been a conscious decision till then. She'd merely acted on instinct—an instinct which compelled her to forget about being Connor Lawrence's nanny. She was Ally Fraser, alone with the man she loved and, in spite of the wild alarm bells ringing in her head, she was going to teach him to love her again.

CHAPTER EIGHT

ALLY swam closer to Fletcher.

Treading water, he watched her approach. His eyes remained locked with hers and there was an unreadable expression, a fierce concentration in his gaze, which brought colour to her cheeks, despite the temperature of the river. She could almost sense his driving need for her to close the final, short gap between them.

'The water's colder than I expected,' she said with a forced smile as she reached him.

'It doesn't take long to get used to it.' His voice was thick and even deeper than normal.

Self-consciously she added, 'It's the best way to cool off after a long, hot day.'

He grinned and his eyes sparkled expectantly, but he made no move.

The pink and orange lights of late afternoon danced across the rippling water, bathing his skin in a golden glow, enhancing his hard-muscled male beauty.

Oh, how she loved him. If only... But now was not the time for wishing. Action was required.

Without allowing herself time for second thoughts, she swam over to him and placed her hands boldly on his shoulders. With only a moment's hesitation, he crushed her to him, his lips closing on hers with a breathless hunger.

Cool water encircled them as his body told her the truth. There was absolutely no doubt that he wanted her. He lowered his head to kiss her throat and shoulders; his lips caressing while his hands moulded her tightly against

his strength. Ally felt herself arch towards him provocatively in a fever pitch of need.

'Dear Ally. What a little temptress you are.'

Just to prove the statement, she kissed him back,
deeply, daringly. Then she ducked out of his arms and
began to swim back towards the bank. Her smile widened
as he caught her easily and rolled her over in the water,
playfully drawing her slim body against him and kissing
her once more, his tongue exploring the inner softness of
her mouth.

She heard a strange, animal sound rumble in her throat.
And he echoed her need with a hungry growl, holding
her head in both hands so that he could kiss her thoroughly, possessively.

A deep, primitive tremor shook through her body. At
that moment she didn't care that he might soon remember
who she was and once more evict her from his property.
For now, in his arms, she could forget everything except
that Fletcher wanted her and she wanted him.

Gently, he guided her back towards the bank. Glorious
sensations were building up, driving her to cling to him,
her body meshed with his, begging a closer intimacy. Her
breasts pushed through the filmy swimsuit into the hairy
wall of his chest. Fletcher lifted her out of the water to
kiss each aching nipple through the thin, wet fabric and
a loud moan burst from her lips. Then she felt the rough
sand under her feet and realised they had reached the
shallows. Urgently, Ally slipped the clinging bathers
from her shoulders to reveal her breasts, wet and gleaming in the fading light and swollen with desire.

'Oh, sweet heaven, Ally. What are you doing to me?'

'I want you,' she answered, her voice pleading.
She was a siren, a water nymph, heady with a desire
that endured since time began. Her lover was a tall,
bronzed god.

'You're divine,' he whispered back, drawing a line with his finger down her throat and across her quivering skin, to trace the outline of a nipple, taut with need for him.

Then he froze and a puzzled expression slipped over his features before he stepped back abruptly. For a long, tortuous moment, Fletcher stared at her. He was about to speak, to touch her again when he turned abruptly, and left her to gaze mutely at his back and buttocks as he strode up the bank.

Ally remained in the ankle-deep water, stunned and shivering, hardly aware of whether it was the evening air or his rejection that caused the sudden chill to invade her entire body. Dimly, she was conscious of Fletcher drying himself roughly with a towel he'd snatched from the back of the Rover and dragging jeans back over his long limbs.

And as he made his way back down the bank towards her, the towel slung around his bare shoulders, her first reaction was to become embarrassed, crossing her arms over her bared breasts, but her humiliation quickly turned to anger. How could he do this to her? The Fletcher she knew could never have been so cruel and he would never have had the strength of will to walk away from what she so generously offered.

Too soon, he reached the sandy ledge at the bottom of the bank, and a stab of icy fear sliced through her when she saw the glazed shock in his eyes.

Had he remembered? Is that why he walked away?

He stepped towards her, his eyes dark, reflecting deep pain. 'Ally. I'm so sorry. Please, let me explain.'

His voice was so considerate, so tender, that she found herself calming in spite of her apprehension. He handed her the towel, with which she immediately covered herself, then she stepped back, her head haughtily high. If there was one thing she could resurrect from this disaster, it would be her dignity.

'It's so strange,' he began hesitantly. 'I wanted you so badly, and then, just as I was going almost out of mind with desire, I had this terrible feeling, a conviction if you like, that I—that before I lost my memory, I was already committed to someone.'

He stared down at her with a bewildered, shy smile. Her heart pounded with accelerated speed as she took in what he was saying.

'You mean you—you think there's somebody else?'

'Well, I can't bloody remember anybody else,' he exclaimed with a frustrated grimace, 'but there's this feeling that—well, I don't exactly know, but, until I get my damned memory back, I think I shouldn't get too involved. I guess it sounds pretty weird, but I kind of feel as if I may already be in love with someone.'

You are, you great galoot, she wanted to scream. You're madly, deeply in love with me!

'I'm sorry, Ally. I should have thought of this before. I shouldn't have started this.' Here he was again, just like in Melbourne, apologising for loving her, when it was all she wanted him to do. 'But if there is someone else—well, I've never believed in two-timing. Do you understand?'

His expression was so intense, pleading with her, that she felt a queer, quiet exhilaration spread through her. If only Fletcher could remember how much he loved her! Slowly her intense disappointment was overtaken by a tingling dawning of hope.

The hopeful feeling stayed with her all evening as they lit the camp fire, cooked crispy, homemade sausages stuffed with herbs, onions and tomatoes in an old, blackened frying pan and boiled the billy, throwing in a good handful of tea leaves to be stirred with a gum tree twig.

Above them, a sliver of moon painted the bush and the murmuring river with a thin, white light as, slowly, the stars emerged in the smooth, black sky. Even when the mournful cry of a curlew reached them from further downriver, Ally continued to nurse the little ball of hope deep within her.

She thought briefly of the glittering hotels and theatres and busy streets of Melbourne at night, lit by the headlights of thousands of cars and flashing neon signs. And she realised that her life in the south now seemed strangely distant, vague and not quite real—like something she had seen on television. This bush was her reality now. She was sure she understood Fletcher's feeling for the land. Her family might not have owned the land for generations, but she still loved it. She loved the slim, white trunks of the eucalypts as they gleamed in the moonlight, the moody river returning back to its usual sleepy languor, the glowing camp fire crackling contentedly. And, of course, she loved it because this was where Fletcher belonged.

They sat by the fire on their rolled-out swags and after they drank their tea, Fletcher leaned over and took Ally's mug. 'Let me get you some real bush tucker,' he said with a grin.

She watched in silence as he walked over to the vehicle and pulled out a bottle from which he poured a small slug into each mug. Then he added some water from the canvas sheathed bottle and came back to crouch beside her.

'Rum and river water. Best nightcap for the bush.'

'Rum? Fletcher, I don't think I—'

'Just give it a go. Think of it as good medicine.'

Ally took a tentative sip. The rum was strong, fiery and sweet at the same time.

'I guess I could get used to it,' she said, smiling.

A blackened log cracked loudly and fell down into the glowing embers. Fletcher stretched out a leather-booted foot to kick it further into the middle of the fire.

In the firelight, his tanned skin took on a ruddy tinge and his thick, black hair, rumpled and unbrushed, gave him a wild, untamed look. It took all of Ally's willpower not to reach out and touch that hair or to place her hand against his bristly cheek, but somehow she stayed still, sipping the rum and trying to stare at the fire rather than the rugged, masculine form beside her. But if she couldn't reach him physically, the need to make emotional contact grew overpowering.

'This girl you might be in love with,' Ally began nervously, 'when do you think you will remember her?'

Fletcher took a deep swig from his mug, his eyes fixed determinedly on the bright flames. 'Can't say. Doctors said it could be a couple of weeks. It's so damn annoying,' he said with a frustrated sigh, 'like I've been put on ice for six months and the world's kept on going without me or—or like I'm missing some vital pieces in a jigsaw puzzle.'

'I wonder how it will happen,' Ally went on, a strange, masochistic force urging her to persist. 'It must be strange to get your memory back. I wonder if it will happen slowly with little snippets of memory popping into your mind here and there or whether it'll come all in a rush.' She curled her legs beneath her and leant towards Fletcher.

She had absolutely no idea how appealing she looked, her slim, lithe body bathed in dancing firelight, her dark hair falling softly to frame her pale face.

'I guess I'll wake up one morning and—hey presto! The missing pieces will fit back in the jigsaw.'

'But I wonder how you'll actually remember her...this girl you think you're in love with...'

'If she exists—' Fletcher interrupted.

'Well, okay, just assuming she does exist. I wonder what you'll remember first.'

Fletcher turned from the fire then to stare at Ally, his dark brows meeting over blue eyes.

'You mean, will I, for example, remember her voice first?'

'Yes, or—or perhaps the colour of her...hair.'

'Or her eyes,' he added slowly, gazing deep into Ally's eyes as if he were seeing them for the first time. She looked away quickly, afraid she might be tempting fate. If his memory were to return now, her gamble could lose out. And yet, morbid curiosity compelled her to press dangerously on.

'Maybe it'll be an event—something you did together,' she suggested to the flames.

There was a long pause while the only sound was the quiet crackle of the fire.

'Like a kiss, Ally, is that what you mean?'

Ally felt her blushing reaction rising swiftly.

'Perhaps, I will remember making love to her,' said Fletcher, his voice rumbling suggestively, causing a wave of impulsive desire to sweep through Ally so strongly she almost cried out. 'I might remember her soft, round breasts or her silky thighs...'

Looking quickly at Fletcher, she found his eyes challenging her as she sensed a similar need pulsing through him. He was swallowing rapidly and grasping the chipped enamelled mug so tightly that his knuckles were white.

Uncomfortably aware of the sudden blaze of pure chemistry sizzling between them, Ally bent forward and picked up a twig to throw into the fire.

Fletcher's gaze followed the sweep of her hand as it

tossed the stick. 'Or it could be some little thing about the beautiful way she moves...' he said softly.

Startled, she looked at him.

'I think it's very noble of you to—to be faithful to her,' she said forcefully.

'Well I don't really think there's much nobility involved,' he replied with a rueful grin, 'it's just that I'd hate all the explanations if things got too complicated. That's the way I am. You see, I couldn't lie to anyone— not to her or to you.'

As Fletcher threw his head back to drain the last of the rum, Ally felt guilt prowl up her back and wrap its clammy hands around her throat.

You had to lie, she reassured herself. He left you no alternative. He'll understand when the time comes.

Miserably she watched as Fletcher put his mug down and said, 'Enough of this. Time to catch some shut-eye. I want to make an early start in the morning.'

He took both mugs over to the truck and returned carrying two thick jumpers. 'It can get really chilly, especially in the early morning just before dawn.'

'Thanks,' gulped Ally. She stood looking down at the swags—two big, khaki green canvas envelopes lined with checked woollen blankets. They were so glaringly self-sufficient. Not what she'd had in mind at all.

During the journey out, she had imagined that she would spend the night in the warmth and safety of Fletcher's arms, but there was a considerable gap of leaf-strewn dirt between the two swags.

And now, she felt just a little nervous of the great expanse of pitch-black bush which stretched all around them just outside the small circle of firelight.

'Is anything the matter, Ally?'

Of course there is. I want to be sleeping with you. Not all neatly tucked up and alone. I want you to pull me down beside you and wrap your gorgeous body up with mine. I want you to check out my breasts, my silky thighs. I want you, Fletcher. I love you. I need you. I need you now, tonight and every night.

'I was just hoping Connor got to sleep okay,' she said softly.

Fletcher banked up the fire. 'He'll be fine. Mary was tickled pink to have him to herself.'

Ally got into the swag and lay stiffly, staring at the night sky. The myriad of stars, pinned to a black satin background, stared back at her like thousands of blinking, uncaring eyes. Ally miserably acknowledged that it was going to be a long night. And in the vast, remote depths of the universe she, and her petty little needs, rated as insignificant. Tonight, even the moon, which sometimes looked so golden and friendly, had reduced itself to a thin, cold slice of silver and, in callous disregard of her loneliness, it trailed its meagre light across the river with a ghostly finger.

Fletcher lay with his back to her. It was difficult to tell if he was asleep, but he looked very relaxed and comfortable, without any sign of the tense, nerve-tingling anxiety she was experiencing. A mopoke called suddenly from a nearby tree, frightening her, and she thought of snakes and wondered if they would dare to crawl anywhere near her when she was so close to the fire.

She rolled onto her side so that she lay facing the fire instead of the night sky. She'd heard of the mesmerising effects of staring into the flames. If she watched them flicker and didn't let herself think about the man nearby, perhaps she would fall asleep.

It must have worked because the next thing she knew was the sound of an axe chopping wood and she woke to find the fire almost out and the bush filled with the pale, creamy light of dawn. On the river below, a fine, white mist was trailing along the surface of the water. Some distance beyond the camp, Fletcher, bare-chested, wielded his axe at a fallen log with astonishing ease, his muscles flexing rhythmically with each movement.

He stopped, bundled the chopped wood under one arm, swung the axe over his shoulder and walked back to their fireplace with long, effortless strides.

'Did you sleep well?' he asked as he dropped the logs and bent to remake the fire.

'Yes, I did actually,' she replied, not hiding her surprise.

'Must have been the rum,' he said with a grin. 'Now, you stay there and relax while I rustle up some breakfast. How about some nice unhealthy bacon and eggs?'

'Sounds great.' She smiled, enjoying the way he set to preparing breakfast with boyish enthusiasm.

After breakfast, they set off for what Fletcher called the back-country. This was rougher land and for hours they wound their way in and out of the foothills of range country where many cattle had virtually gone wild.

'A lot of cleanskins in here,' Fletcher told her. 'Cattle that've never been branded. We'll bring in a helicopter to chase them out of these nooks and then later the men on the ground will take over.'

By late afternoon, they had reached very different country. They parked beside a swamp where huge, pink lotus flowers floated on the still surface and above which cruised black and white magpie geese. From the swamp they walked upstream and as they climbed, the water grew clearer and faster flowing.

'It's actually spring fed,' said Fletcher. 'This water comes bubbling out of the basalt further up.'

Ally noticed that the vegetation was changing as well and soon they reached a pocket of rainforest thick with lilly pilly trees and wild bananas.

'This is another favourite spot of mine,' he said. 'There's something here I want to show you,' he added, taking her hand and leading her along a faint wallaby track through the forest.

They reached the prettiest creek Ally had ever seen. The water was so clear she could see every round, smooth pebble on the bottom. Soft, green ferns and baby palms lined its banks while mossy logs or smooth stepping stones provided comfortable seats to rest and take in the tranquil beauty.

'Let's sit back a bit on the bank,' whispered Fletcher. 'If we're very patient, we might just see something pretty special.'

'Not a platypus?' squeaked Ally, incredulously. 'I've never seen one.'

'Ssh!' said Fletcher, and he crouched low, pulling Ally beside him till they were both sitting close together on a fallen log. Hardly daring to breathe, Ally sat perfectly still beside Fletcher and kept her eyes roving up and down the creek with intense concentration. All through the rainforest, the late afternoon shadows were lengthening. In the canopy above, birds were busy calling to each other, but there was no other sound except the quiet chuckle of the water as it bubbled over rocks.

Ally began to grow stiff from sitting so still and she wriggled a little. Fletcher stilled her with a strong hand on her arm. Slowly he pointed downstream. In the dim light, Ally could just make out a little brown form moving upstream towards them, close to the river bank. A thrill of excitement surged through her. As it drew closer, she could hear the little splashing sounds it made as it snuffled its bill through the soft mud on the creek bottom. Hardly bigger than Fletcher's hand, the platypus dived and resurfaced, busily hunting and feeding in the twilight creek.

Just in front of them, it stopped and looked at something on the bank. Still as a statue, Ally's thrilled eyes drank in every quaintly absurd detail—the little flat paddling tail, the round furry abdomen, ducklike bill and flippers and beady little brown eyes, ringed with gold. It only paused for a few moments and then it was off again, sifting the bottom of the creek, hunting for worms and beetles like a busy shopper, hurrying to get the ingredients for supper before the shops closed.

Eventually it disappeared around a bend in the creek and Ally turned to Fletcher, her face alight. 'That was just fabulous!' she cried and threw her arms around him in a spontaneous hug. 'A platypus! All my life I've wanted to see a live one in the wild. Oh, thank you so much, Fletcher, I feel so honoured. We'll have to bring Connor here and show him.'

He smiled as he gave her a return hug, but then he drew back and looked down into her face, his hands still resting on her shoulders and his happiness was replaced by a more serious, disturbing expression. 'It was an honour to share it with you,' he said softly and bent his head to touch his lips to the tip of her nose.

Ally caught her breath.

'Stop looking at me like that,' he whispered.

'How, Fletcher?' she asked lamely.

'Like you want to be in my bed.'

Ally gulped and felt a hot tide of colour sweep over her. 'I—I...' What could she say? He was right and he knew it.

His hand gently caressed her face, sliding beneath the curtain of her silky, dark hair to stroke the nape of her neck while he kissed her eyelids and her chin. His other hand slowly pressed into her spine, feeling her shudder with longing as he drew her closer.

'We shouldn't be doing this,' whispered Fletcher and he left a trail of feather-light kisses down her neck.

'No,' agreed Ally, wrapping her arms more tightly around him and murmuring against his cheek. 'That other girl mightn't like it.'

'Maybe she wouldn't mind just…' Fletcher tasted her lips, moving his mouth over hers in a soft caress, then drew back '…a little kiss,' he whispered.

'I'm sure she wouldn't,' replied Ally, and in case Fletcher had any further doubts, she clung to him, her mouth avidly seeking his.

It was a deep, hungry kiss, fed by the longing that had consumed her for days. Breathless, they broke apart at last, only to laugh shakily and seek each other again. And then Fletcher's kisses became even more urgent. He crushed her against him and took her mouth in fierce, starved passion. Ally felt happiness bubbling from deep inside her and surrendered completely to his male dominance, letting herself drown in the wonder of being back in his arms, of the glory of his mouth as she opened her lips wider to welcome him.

She moaned under his onslaught. 'Oh, Fletcher, oh yes, please.' Her pleas excited him further, urging him to kiss her again with feverish savagery, raining kisses on her eyes, her throat, his hands cupping and teasing her breasts, his breath coming in short, gasping moans.

Ally returned his kisses ardently, almost biting him in her desperate need to be a part of him. 'Oh, Fletcher,' she groaned. 'I love you so much.' Her eager words sounded suddenly loud in the quiet bush and to her mortification, she felt Fletcher draw back.

He was panting and his wild, darkened eyes revealed an intense yearning. But he sighed and, taking her hand, he kissed each of her fingers in turn.

'Unfortunately,' he murmured, 'if we don't get back

to our vehicle before dark, we might get ourselves lost or at the very least break a leg among the basalt rocks. We've no food, torch or matches in here. It would be a long, cold night.'

Who cares? Ally wanted to cry, but she had to acknowledge that all around them, the bush was growing much darker. Long shadows were already making the track quite hard to see. Reluctantly, she drew away from Fletcher. 'If you insist on being practical, I guess we'd better go back,' she replied, pretending to grumble.

'Let's hurry,' he murmured breathlessly. 'I don't think I can stay practical for long.'

They sprang up and made their way quickly down the track, like excited children.

Ally knew her smile was as wide as the plains they'd travelled over. Her imagination danced with excited possibilities. She had never felt so quietly confident that all would be well, so deliciously expectant. As she walked lightly beside Fletcher, she felt utterly peaceful, and enveloped by a warm hopeful glow. Fletcher could surely not resist her again tonight. He was clearly very attracted to her. He seemed to like Ally the nanny as passionately as he'd liked Ally the fashion designer. She felt a growing confidence that when he discovered they were both the same person, he would be doubly pleased.

But it was more than a physical hunger they shared. On this journey, as they'd enjoyed the tranquil beauty of the bush, the plains and the rainforest, they had experienced a special closeness, a complete understanding that came from something much deeper than basic lust.

They made their way as quickly as possible, following the stream back down the hillside. As the track thinned, Ally walked ahead of him a little with eager, skipping steps, her heart light, thinking of the night ahead and the promise conveyed in his passionate kisses. They had almost reached the bottom, when the ground began to level out and the track widened once more into a small clearing bordered by wild bananas and a creeper covered in round yellow fruit.

'Are these edible?' she asked. 'Perhaps we could have some for dessert.'

She sensed Fletcher stop suddenly behind her and turned to see his body stiffen perceptibly.

'They're wild passionfruit,' he said quietly.

'Really?' she replied, trying to still the sudden savage beating in her chest. Why had Fletcher's answer felt like a physical blow?

'They taste the same as the cultivated variety except that they're not...'

He paused and Ally wished for all the world she could stop him from saying what had to come next.

'...Purple. These passionfruit aren't purple,' Fletcher repeated softly. It was even darker now, but Ally could see the bleak expression on his face and she could hear the subtle change in his voice.

He spoke again, very slowly and quite coldly. 'Passionfruit.' Then he stepped towards her in a stiff, broken manner, as if he'd been struck from behind. 'Ally,' he whispered. 'Ally, it's you, isn't it?'

'What—what are you talking about, Fletch?' she asked, her voice shaking with growing fear. But she knew.

He had remembered.

'Oh, hell! Damn you, Ally.' Fletcher ground out the words. Pushing her roughly aside, he strode past her.

Horrified, Ally stumbled after him, almost falling in her haste. She reached out to grab at his arm.

'Fletch, wait! What is it? What's the matter?'

He turned and scowled down at her, wild-eyed. 'How

can you pretend you don't know, you scheming little liar.'

'Fletch, you've got it all wrong. I didn't really mean to trick you.'

But he strode away from her, his face twisted in anger and his shoulders hunched forward aggressively.

Running to catch up, Ally grabbed at his arm once more and sobbed at him to stop. She stood, panting, tears streaming down her face. 'I'm sorry, Fletcher,' she said. 'I really am. It was wrong of me to—to not tell you the whole truth. Please, please forgive me.'

For a fraction of a second she thought she saw a softening of his grim features. He looked down at her, breathing savagely. His eyes searched her face wildly and she put a tentative hand on his arm pleadingly, but then he shook her off.

'How could you do it, Ally? If it wasn't almost night, I'd be driving you straight back to the homestead now,' he roared hoarsely. 'Instead, we leave at first light. And this time, you are going home to Melbourne and there won't be any floods to stop you.'

CHAPTER NINE

A FEW more angry strides brought them out of the scrub and back to the parked truck. Fletcher grabbed the axe straight away, muttering something about firewood.

'Fletcher, we've got to talk about this. I've apologised. A few minutes ago we were kissing for heaven's sake. You didn't want me to leave then.' Even as Ally spoke, the memory of his urgent desire gave her courage.

'A few minutes ago I didn't know you were betraying my trust.'

She flinched, stepping back, as she felt the bitterness of his words hit her.

'You know,' she began, but her voice cracked. She took a deep breath and tried again, not at all sure where her pride had gone or why she persisted, but knowing there was only one way for her to survive now and that was to fight back with whatever weapon happened to be at her disposal. Unfortunately, all she had left was the truth. 'You know I love you. You must know why I came here.'

His eyes, sad and angry, met hers fleetingly and then he looked at the ground between them. 'You can't stay here, Ally. There's no place here for you in the outback.' He lifted the axe and shook it at her and then, with a bewildered expression, seemed to realise what he was doing and put the axe down on the grass beside him.

'You made that pretty clear once before. But, Fletcher, you're wrong. I can stay here. I have stayed here. I stayed on and I fitted in,' Ally countered.

He stepped towards her and grabbed her shoulders with

both hands, shaking her angrily. 'Why are you so stubborn? You must go back to the city. I don't want you here.'

'That's rubbish and you know it,' Ally fired back.

A wary gleam flickered in Fletcher's eyes but he insisted fiercely, 'It's absolute common sense, Ally. It's totally impractical for you to consider living on Wallaroo Downs. It just won't work.'

'Why not?'

'Why not? It's glaringly obvious.'

'Not to me it isn't.'

'Ally, what's happened to your vision, your ambition?'

'It's very clear,' she replied softly. 'It's just shifted focus, that's all.'

Fletcher stared at her, his face pale and drawn. For a moment she thought she'd connected, that he finally understood just how serious she was, but his next words dashed her almost-extinguished hope.

'I've let you stay on here because you conned me into believing you were suitable, but there's no way I want you staying on now I know the truth.'

'You—you're not a very good actor, Fletcher.'

His blue eyes darkened formidably. 'Acting? Don't kid yourself. I've never been more serious in my life.'

He reached for the axe again and heaved it onto his shoulder, turning to walk away. There was no way she was going to accept this without a fight. Not now when she was sure he really did love her. Desperate, Ally ran up to Fletcher and stopped him by planting both hands firmly in the middle of his huge chest.

'What went wrong? What changed after you left Melbourne? Why are you doing this to me?'

He shrugged her off as if she were a bothersome insect and headed for some fallen timber a few metres away. Ally followed.

'This is getting a touch monotonous. I have my own lifestyle here and you just don't fit in. As I said before, you should never have come chasing me out here, Ally. I tried to make a clean break, when I realised what a serious mistake we were making...' He swung the axe high above his head. 'Step back,' he warned. 'You should also never stand in front of a man with an axe, especially in this poor light.'

Ally stepped away quickly as the axe smashed down, splintering the timber and sending little pieces flying. Mistake...the word buzzed in her head. So she was a mistake?

'Why don't you come straight out and tell me what's wrong with me,' she yelled as he eased the axe out of the timber it had split. He paused and glared at her.

'You lied,' he said coolly.

'But, even before that, when I was being completely honest, you wanted to get rid of me then, too.'

He straightened and the blue eyes regarded her for ten seconds as if he were remembering and piecing together the details of the other time he tried to evict her. She capitalised on his hesitation.

'How much do you really remember, Fletcher? Perhaps you have forgotten how strong our feelings were. Even now, you say you don't want me, but, heavens above, your body tells me something else. You do want me, Fletcher—just as much as I want you. We can't just ignore what we had before. How can you just pretend that nothing happened?'

His jaw tightened. 'For your information, I do remember everything—unfortunately. You can have no doubt of that.' His shoulders stiffened as if he was gathering strength before he spoke again. 'It may have been special for you, but you've no idea how I felt.'

'Don't I?' she spat back. 'You showed me how you

felt when you kissed me back there. And yesterday in
the river,' she added with a sudden surge of confidence.
'You said then that you were already in love with somebody. Well, here I am.'

The simplicity of her logic took him aback. Fletcher
stared at her for at least a minute, his hand clasping and
unclasping the axe and he gave a little negative shake of
his head as if she had almost convinced him, but when
his eyes fixed on hers again, he spoke with biting calm.
'Ally, face the facts. What we share isn't love. Love and
all that it involves—sharing a future together—requires
a compatibility of many dimensions, not just an unfortunately strong sexual magnetism. I don't think I ever
claimed to be in love, but remember I was suffering from
amnesia. I obviously got it wrong.'

The battle was over.

Ally cringed, eyes closed, hands shaking, facing defeat. She had stubbornly refused to see the startlingly
obvious. All this time she had continued to believe in
romantic dreams of love and commitment, when, as far
as Fletcher was concerned, all they had ever shared was
straightforward lust. She had to admit he had never pretended otherwise.

She had failed.

He raised the axe again. 'Now, if you don't let me
chop this firewood, we'll have no light and no warmth
and no dinner. We're in for a wretched night anyhow,
but let's at least make it a bit comfortable.'

She had failed completely. Ally backed away across
the clearing, watching him begin to chop the wood with
reckless energy. The sun had almost set and the sky behind Fletcher was navy blue streaked with blood red. The
air was cooler than the night before so she gave no
thought to another swim. He chopped the wood quickly
and brought it over, nearer to the camp.

'This do for the fireplace?' he asked.

Ally shrugged, wishing she could just tell him to drop dead, but she had lost the will to fight. Walking around to the other side of the vehicle, she hauled out the swags and dumped them on the dusty ground.

Fletcher came over and checked the contents of the esky. 'What would you like for dinner?' he asked politely. 'How about a steak?'

'I'm not really hungry,' she muttered.

He chose to ignore her petulance and carried two large steaks over to the pan, which was already heating on the fire. He sliced some tomatoes and opened a tin of mushrooms to heat up for the steaks. Then he snapped the tops off two beers and offered her one. 'They're not very cold anymore,' he said. 'The ice has just about melted.'

Ally took the proffered can and when she flinched from the touch of his hand against hers, Fletcher froze briefly, his face a blank mask. Looking away, Ally leaned back against the truck's tyre and took a long gulp of beer. She'd never really enjoyed beer all that much, but her throat was dry and the liquid wet and cool. Her throat seemed to be the only part of her body with any feeling. The rest of her felt strangely numb, desolate.

Nothing had worked out as she had hoped. This whole venture had been a monumental failure. But her mind wouldn't let go of the puzzling fact that one minute, Fletcher could kiss her hungrily as if he needed her desperately, and then in virtually the next breath, he could claim that he never wanted to see her again. Love and lust. How many other poor fools had confused those two? She had been so ecstatic in his arms, revelling in his kisses, sure that he had never stopped loving her. But then he had so effortlessly stifled the last tiny shred of hope.

Maybe it hadn't been quite effortless, she conceded as

she thought about the pain in his eyes as his memory relentlessly returned. Watching him glumly as he hunkered down over the fire, turning the steaks, Ally wondered again if there wasn't a more complicated reason for his rejection of her.

He was prepared to be very interested in her living here when he thought she was a nanny from central Queensland, but had absolutely no interest when he discovered she was a fashion designer from Victoria. She had never really accepted Lucette's warning that he had very fixed ideas about what kind of woman belonged in the bush, but obviously his cousin was spot-on.

The bottom line was that she had failed miserably. She had tried to win him by fair means and she'd tried deception. Neither had worked and now she had no alternative but to do as he asked—to leave Wallaroo Downs and return to the city where she would be greeted by raised eyebrows and knowing smirks and the news that her contracts had been passed on to other designers. Terrific!

Her mind churned furiously. Like a cat unable to leave a mouse, her relentless mind toyed with every possible way to examine her plight. She tried to put herself in his position. If he had arrived on the doorstep of her Melbourne flat and announced that he'd sold Wallaroo Downs and was planning to find a job in the city, she would have been shocked and outraged, too. She would never have wanted him to make himself miserable, giving up the country and the work he loved for her. Definitely not. But she would have been touched by his willingness to sacrifice everything for her. Wouldn't she? Just what would she have done? The more she tried to unravel her thoughts, the more impossible the problem seemed to become.

The night was as long and as wretched as Fletcher had

predicted. Ally ate very little of the juicy steak and later, although she stared into the flames once again, they had no more power to lull her to sleep than a pack of dingoes howling around their camp. The ground beneath her felt hard and rocky. Mosquitoes circled and dive-bombed repeatedly despite the smoke from the fire. Ally lay tense and miserable, watching the flames gradually die down until only the big logs and the ashes beneath them glowed red. With weary eyes, she traced the journey of the Southern Cross from the horizon as it climbed up the sky and her ears strained, listening to the silence of the wilderness which grew more menacing with every passing hour.

She suspected Fletcher was not sleeping too well, either. He tossed and turned several times and there was no regular, soft breathing to indicate sleep.

They were both up as soon as the first glimmer of dawn tinged the eastern sky, as if neither of them wanted to stay in the swags a moment longer. Fletcher's face looked strained and weary and Ally was sure hers must be worse. They both agreed that a mug of tea would be sufficient for breakfast and before the sun was completely up, they were packed. They took the most direct route heading straight for Wallaroo homestead. It was a difficult, tense journey, long and hot with virtually no stops.

Both were wrapped in their own thoughts. Ally's were desolate. She had no choice but to do as Fletcher asked—demanded. And she dreaded the thought of explaining to Connor why she had to go.

She was completely exhausted by the time the long, low roof of the homestead, surrounded by its circle of ancient trees, appeared on the horizon and she knew that, after driving for hours, Fletcher must be ready to drop.

When they reached the yard, Ned was already there. On hearing their vehicle approach, he'd hobbled out of one of the machinery sheds to open the last gate and he didn't attempt to hide a knowing grin when he saw their sleep-deprived faces.

'What's amusing you?' Fletcher snapped.

'Just pleased to see you back, boss,' Ned replied quickly, the smile disappearing fast. Then he added smartly, 'You've got visitors.'

'You're joking,' Fletcher groaned.

'No. It's Tom and Ruth Neville and their littl'uns. They came over to meet Ally and Connor.' After delivering his message, Ned hobbled away quickly, clearly uncertain of his boss's reaction to the news.

Ally stole a look at Fletcher's expression and was relieved to hear him chuckle in laughing disbelief. 'There's fate for you,' he sighed as he dragged a hand through his matted hair. 'They're my neighbours from Mungulla Station. Actually,' he added with a wry grimace, 'I told them to come over and meet you both anytime they liked. But they've got lousy timing.'

Ally regarded him for a long moment. 'I guess, even though they're neighbours, they spent most of the day getting here.'

'Exactly.'

'So you can't tell them sorry, come again another day.'

'Well, of course I could, but the Nevilles and I go back a long way. But for heaven's sake, tonight of all nights!'

They both sat staring ahead through the dust-spattered windscreen.

'Nevertheless you wouldn't want to spoil a good friendship.'

'Not if I can avoid it.'

'Then it's settled then.' Ally turned up her palms and twisted her features into something approaching a smile. 'I'll behave myself if that's what you're worried about. I won't turn on any tantrums.'

Fletcher nodded grimly. 'This doesn't change a thing, Ally. You'll still have to go.'

'Of course,' she sniffed and, reaching to the cabin floor, she picked up her carryall. 'I'll get the esky out of the back and take it in to Mary.' She opened the car door and got out, closing it forcefully behind her. 'See you later,' she called as he began to drive towards the garage. He turned to look at her, but said nothing and drove on.

When Ally reached the kitchen, she was grateful to find it empty. Mechanically, she unpacked the few perishables they had not used and stacked them in the refrigerator, disposing of the one or two items that were beyond salvage. Then she rinsed out the esky, left it upturned on the draining board, and hurried quickly to her room. Her number one priority was a long, hot shower.

She also longed to sleep, but at least the shower helped to soothe her exhausted body. After the dust and smoke of the camp and the sweat of the long journey, soap had never smelled so good. Showered and a little refreshed, she brushed her clean hair and changed into comfortable silk-knit slacks and top and wondered if Fletcher had been able to enjoy a clean up, as well.

Stop thinking about him! she admonished herself. He's not yours to care about and the sooner you accept that idea the better. But she knew it was no use. Learning to stop loving Fletcher was going to take her a long, long time. She didn't know if it was ever possible.

'Ally!'

A little bundle of four-year-old boy hurtled through her doorway and hugged her tight.

'Connor, darling. How's my big boy?'

'We've got visitors,' the child announced importantly.

'So I hear. Where are they?' At that moment, Ally heard a little giggle and then another. She looked over Connor's shoulder to see two little girls peering around the door. They had identical round faces covered in freckles, topped by bright red hair. Their brown eyes were enormous.

'They're twins,' whispered Connor.

'I see,' agreed Ally. 'Are you going to introduce me to your friends?'

'Katie and Lissa,' he said shyly, but his eyes were glowing.

'Melissa,' corrected one of the little girls boldly, entering the room and addressing Ally. 'That's my sister. Connor can't say her name properly yet, 'cause he's only four.'

'We're five,' contributed Melissa.

'Hello, Katie and Melissa. It's lovely to meet you.'

'We're going to start school of the air next year,' added Melissa, emboldened by Ally's warm smile.

'Connor, isn't this lovely to have some friends to play with? What have you been doing?'

'He's been showing us his pony,' interrupted Katie, her eyes widening even further. 'He's so lucky. We don't have our own ponies yet and we're bigger'n Connor.'

'But Daddy says we might buy two from Uncle Fletcher at Christmas time,' added her twin, not to be outdone. Then she turned to Connor excitedly. 'We usually come over here for Christmas and have a big party.'

The little boy smiled happily and squeezed Ally's hand.

'Won't that be nice,' whispered Ally, stifling the cold wave of despair that threatened when she thought of them all celebrating Christmas without her.

Where would she be by Christmas? Back in Melbourne, sitting in her apartment, alone. At the mere thought of her neat Melbourne home, surrounded by other city apartments with their pristine urban gardens, devoid of scraggy eucalyptus trees, wildlife, creeks or mountains, she felt an overwhelming sense of loss. For a while she had tasted a different life, been in a different world and, while the major draw card had been Fletcher Hardy, the unique beauty of the outback had won her heart as well. Now she would have to leave the bush and there was nothing she could do about it.

'Is this where you've got to?' A feminine voice broke into Ally's thoughts. She turned to see a smiling woman standing in the doorway. 'Hi, you must be Ally. Sorry they've barged in on you like this. What are you scallywags doing invading this poor woman's bedroom?'

'They're fine,' smiled Ally, liking instantly the other woman's laughing face, and her friendly manner. 'You must be Mrs. Neville.'

'Oh, please. You must call me Ruth.'

Ruth Neville, Ally guessed, was in her mid-thirties, around the same age as her sister, and, like Victoria, she had the calm, happy air of a wife and mother who loved her family and who was loved in return. Blond, suntanned and with minimal make-up, she looked smart yet comfortable in a slim-fitting blue linen shift and strappy sandals.

'Now, come on, you lot. We'll leave Ally a chance to catch her breath before dinner. We can talk to her as much as we like then.' She turned to Ally. 'Take your time,' she said. 'No need at all to rush.' She bundled the children, Connor included, out onto the veranda. 'Fletcher's only just hit the shower and I can give Mary a hand. See you for dinner at seven.'

Ally watched them leave with a sense of gratitude— an hour or so to rest was exactly what her aching body needed. If only her mind would let go, too.

Fletcher had dressed for dinner in an open-necked, white dress shirt and dark slacks which accentuated his dark, rangy masculinity to a painful degree, and Tom and Ruth had also changed for dinner, so Ally was glad she'd decided to dress up a little. She chose a quiet, pearl-grey crepe, cut in a simple style with thin shoulder straps, fitted bodice and a softly flared skirt. It always made her feel particularly feminine and she needed to feel good about something tonight. She knew the soft grey shade matched her eyes exactly. At the last minute, she added Fletcher's amethyst necklace. But as she entered the dining room and saw Fletcher's face grow pale and taut as his eyes rested on her, she wondered if she had gone too far.

Nevertheless, tired and drawn as he clearly was, Fletcher's innate good manners ensured that he was a charming host. Adults and children all shared the meal at the big table in the dining room. To her surprise, Ally found she was to sit opposite Fletcher at one end of the table, while the Nevilles and Connor were ranged on either side. It looked for all the world like she was the lady of the house and during the meal, her eyes inadvertently locked with Fletcher's so that, for frantic seconds, her mind lost the thread of a conversation.

But if Tom or Ruth Neville noticed, they very adeptly covered up with subtly introduced small talk or by allowing one of the children to distract them at just the right moment.

Tom Neville was a tall redhead who had clearly passed his distinctive colouring on to his daughters. He chatted to Ally about the floods and the property and about her job as a nanny.

'Ruth would never hear of a nanny for our pair,' he said, shaking his head at his wife with an affectionate smile. 'And next year she's planning to teach the twins school, as well.'

'But tell Ally the rest,' interrupted Ruth. 'I used to be

a schoolteacher before Tom sailed into Charters Towers and swept me off my feet,' she explained for Ally's benefit.

'I rescued you from a fate worse than death,' argued Tom. 'Admit it, you'd never go back to living in town now, would you?'

'Well, not until I'm old and grey,' smiled Ruth, her eyes resting lovingly on her husband. Then she turned to Ally. 'Are you enjoying your taste of the outback enough to want to stay?'

Ally felt her face burn. She stared at her food, not daring to look at Fletcher, while the words to answer Ruth's question kept sliding out of her mind before she had time to voice them. The silence was so protracted she began to feel quite faint with apprehension.

Twice Fletcher looked like he was going to say something, but no words emerged. Katie, who had not been listening to the conversation because she was too busy polishing off her ice cream, saved the awkward tension at last.

'Uncle Fletcher, are you going to play the piano for us tonight?'

Ally nearly choked. What next? Fletcher, grazier and bushman extraordinaire, could play the piano? It was a concept that had her reaching for her wineglass. She took a deep swig, and glanced quickly at Fletcher, but he was studiously examining his dessert fork.

'Katie,' interjected Ruth, her warning tone implying she was treading carefully through what she found to be a minefield. 'We agreed not to bother Fletcher tonight.'

'Sorry,' murmured the little girl with a heavy sigh.

'I'll practise up ready for the carols at Christmas,' promised Fletcher, clearly relieved to be let off.

Connor, who had been sitting quietly through the meal,

obviously a little overawed by the constant teatime chatter, suddenly spoke up.

'My mummy had a piano.'

'Did she, dear?' asked Ruth, instantly all motherly concern for the poor little orphaned boy.

Ally observed Connor thoughtfully. This was the first occasion she had actually heard her little charge speak of his mother. She caught Fletcher's eye and a silent message there confirmed that his thoughts echoed her own.

'That's right, Connor,' Fletcher said gently. 'Your mother played the piano beautifully.'

'Can you play "Twinkle Twinkle Little Star"?' Connor looked at his godfather with such a bright, eager expression, Ally could see Fletcher weakening.

'I think I can manage that,' he said with a wry smile.

That settled it. Dessert was finished in an excited flurry, children's hands and faces were washed and everyone except Ally adjourned to the huge room commonly referred to as the ballroom. She stayed behind in the dining room, despite protestations, to help Mary clear the dishes. Somehow, the sight of Fletcher seated at a piano, his huge brown hands moving over the keys, was more than she could bear tonight.

But her ears were riveted to the next room, where she could hear laughter and the first tinkling notes of Connor's request. She loaded a tray with the glassware. Although it was good quality crystal, the care she took was rather more meticulous than necessary, because she found she didn't want to miss one note of Fletcher's playing. Within a few minutes, the simple notes of 'Twinkle, Twinkle' were elaborated and expanded into trills and runs, flourishes and variations, that revealed an astonishing virtuosity.

Stunned, Ally headed for the kitchen with the glass-laden tray, her heart suddenly catapulting. Why, she asked herself, did the thought of Fletcher displaying such prowess at the piano disturb her so much? But she knew the answer. It was so unexpected and yet so right that someone as sensual as he was would have an artistic streak. But why had he hidden it from her? He knew she loved classical music. Together, they had listened to many of her favourite CDs.

Mary, who was at the sink, up to her elbows in dish-water and detergent bubbles turned to her. 'It's lovely to hear him tinkle the old ivories again, isn't it?'

Ally nodded dully. She was saved from having to con-tribute further to the conversation when the music stopped and Ruth Neville came into the kitchen with the children trailing behind her.

'The girls were wondering if Connor could sleep on the veranda with them tonight,' she said. 'Whenever we come here in the summer, they always sleep outside our room on put-up stretchers. They think it's wonderful fun.'

'Would you like that?' Ally asked the little boy quietly.

His shining eyes were answer enough even before he added a fervent, 'Yes, please.'

'Then off with you three to clean your teeth while we make up your beds,' Ruth ordered the delighted trio.

Ruth showed Ally where the folding canvas stretchers were stored and then they raided the linen closet for sheets and pillows. As Ally sorted through the piles to find three pillowslips, Ruth spoke in quiet conspiratorial tones.

'Forgive me for blurting this out, but I've realised who you are,' she said. 'It's been puzzling me all night where I've seen you before, but it's just hit me.'

'Really?' Ally replied. She wasn't alarmed. There had been too many surprises and adjustments to cope with for her to react with anything but resignation.

'You're Alexandra Fraser, the fashion designer, aren't you?'

Ally nodded.

'I'd been admiring your dress all evening. It's so classically simple yet soft,' smiled Ruth. 'Then I remembered reading an article about you and seeing photos of you and your designs in a magazine!'

'That would be right,' sighed Ally.

Ruth stood in the hallway, her arms full of bed linen and her knowing expression lit by an unshaded bulb dangling in front of the still-opened closet.

'I won't pry,' Ruth said, even though she was clearly bursting with curiosity. 'Just let me say I'm absolutely thrilled.'

'You are?' asked Ally weakly, her mind whirling.

'I certainly am. I've known Fletcher for about seven years now and he and Tom grew up together. We both really care about him.'

Ally hugged the bed linen to her chest. She wasn't sure what Ruth was leading to. 'That's great!' she said lamely, her voice shaking.

'You must love Fletcher very, very much.'

'How did you—I mean, um, what makes you think that?' Ally asked, keeping her head lowered.

Ruth laid a gentle hand on Ally's arm. 'Do I really need to explain? It's pretty clear to me. A. You're here. That says heaps. B. I've seen the way you look at him. That tells me more. C. I've seen the way he looks at you. That tells me everything. And that's why I'm so happy. I'm right, am I not?'

'Almost.' Ally hadn't the strength to tell Ruth just how wrong she was.

'That's splendid,' smiled Ruth. 'I have a selfish motive, too, of course. Even though we've just met, I like you, Ally. I'd love to have you as my permanent neighbour. And just think what you could do for the morale of women in the bush if you helped us all to dress as elegantly as you do.'

Ally sighed. The cloak of sadness that had been hovering over her all day seemed to settle solidly on her shoulders and when she spoke, her words were little more than a whisper. 'Well I'm very sorry to disappoint you, Ruth. But I'm not staying. Tomorrow I start packing. I'm going back to Melbourne. For good.'

CHAPTER TEN

'OH, ALLY, why? Why on earth do you have to go?' Ruth looked genuinely disappointed and puzzled. 'I don't know how you came to be here in the first place. I guess it's really none of my business, but I do realise what a sacrifice it must have been.'

'There was a time when I thought coming here was more important than a career,' Ally said softly, aware of the wide-eyed concern in the other woman's eyes.

'Then perhaps it still is. Already you're indispensable.'

Ally wished she could believe that, but she knew that in fact she was easily dispensed with. Whatever niche she'd imagined she could fit into on Wallaroo Downs, had been obliterated with the return of Fletcher's memory.

'Fletcher has no use for me here,' she murmured. Speaking about this was painful; there was a catch in her voice.

'Nonsense,' Ruth insisted. 'If he believes that, he's deluding himself.'

Ally wished she could accept her new friend's reassurance, but Ruth hadn't seen the look on Fletcher's face when he told her she meant nothing to him. She hadn't heard the cold, biting dislike in his voice.

He wanted to be rid of her and the sooner the better.

'One little bit of advice from a former city girl,' Ruth urged. 'If you really want him, and I suspect you do, don't give up, until you're absolutely convinced it will never work.'

It was well-meant advice, but Ally knew she had already reached that conviction. She tried to smile, but it felt twisted and weak. Squaring her shoulders instead, she resolutely suggested that they had better get the children's beds made up.

Gaiety abounded on the veranda as three stretcher beds were lined up and made comfortable for three very excited children. Once they were settled into the beds, a huge mosquito net was hung from a hook high on the veranda wall and then spread to cover them all.

Three little faces were kissed goodnight by both women and then Ruth retired to her bedroom nearby so she could monitor the children's settling down, while Ally went thoughtfully back along the veranda towards her own room. She had almost reached her doorway when a familiar tall, male figure stepped out of the shadows. His eyes, dark as storm-tossed seas, were watching her with a fierce wariness.

'Oh, hello, Fletcher,' she said awkwardly.

'You were talking a long time with Ruth,' he growled.

'Yes, she's a very friendly woman. I like her a lot.'

He looked even more displeased as if he didn't want to hear this. 'Wonderful. I guess you're already the best of mates. I hope this isn't some new tactic you're trying so that you can stay.'

The remark was so unfair, Ally couldn't respond.

'As it happens,' Fletcher said, speaking more calmly. 'It will be difficult for us to leave tomorrow before the Nevilles go, so it will have to be the day after. It means you will have more time to pack. And time to explain to Connor why you must leave.'

How kind and thoughtful, she mused sarcastically before tossing back her reply. 'Thanks for being so considerate.'

Then she pushed past him into her room and pulled

the French doors behind her forcefully, sending the bolt home with a hefty shove.

It was a relief to be able to hate him at last.

Ally stomped around her room, pulling off her clothes, hurling open drawers and kicking off her shoes to remain lying wherever they fell. All she needed was more time to explain to Connor why she was abandoning him!

With an almighty tug she reefed back her bedclothes and flung herself onto the bed. She had no idea how to explain to the little boy that she would be leaving Wallaroo forever. Perhaps, she should only say she was going away for a little while—and gradually he would forget about her.

For hours she tossed and turned and fumed until eventually pure physical exhaustion began to wear her down and finally her anger collapsed into utter misery.

She cried herself to sleep.

It was very late when she woke. She emerged midmorning with a headache from her tears and she was grateful to have escaped breakfast. She was even more pleased that the Neville children were still around to occupy Connor while she set about the dreadful task of packing. And she was thankful that Fletcher, Tom and Ruth appeared to be closeted in the study for most of the morning, busy discussing station business.

Keeping herself as busy as possible, she washed and ironed a huge pile of clothes, vacuumed, dusted and polished her room to within an inch of its life, and packed with great care. It was ridiculous really. She couldn't have cared less what state her clothes were in, but she had to keep busy. The activity couldn't stop her from thinking and feeling utterly miserable, but it used up some of her nervous energy.

She didn't tell Connor she was leaving. She couldn't.

The Nevilles drove off straight after lunch so that they could get back to Mungulla before dark. The children made so much noise calling countless goodbye messages to each other that there was little chance for the adults to do more than exchange polite farewells, but Ruth managed to give Ally a hug and whisper, 'I wouldn't give up yet, if I were you.'

If you knew what I do, I'm sure you would, thought Ally as she waved the chattering family farewell.

Luckily, Connor was happy to have an afternoon nap after the excitement of the past two days and when Ally had finished attending to her things, she started on his, telling herself that it was important that she left his clothes, toys and room spotless for his new nanny.

When he woke, they went for a quiet walk along the creek, and visited the stables to check once again on the pony Fletcher had presented to Connor. Ally kicked fiercely at a tuft of grass as she and the boy walked back across the home paddock, but the action brought no comfort as a light breeze drifted across the summer grass and the afternoon sun tinged the tips of the distant hills with gold.

Her eyes lingered over the scenery surrounding her. The hills, the paddocks, the creek made up this land and it had been lying here, supporting life, for millions of years and would go on doing so for countless more. And she would not be a part of it. She wouldn't be here next time the rains came. She would never take Connor to the platypus creek or swim again in the river at dusk. Fletcher, Connor and the Nevilles would all be here. But she would be gone.

She wouldn't see Connor grow up or Fletcher grow old. Her children would never ride Wallaroo's horses or chase each other along the homestead veranda.

And Fletcher would never again take her in his arms

and hold her tight, needing her passionately. He would never again whisper her name as he kissed her, tasted her, loved her.

'Ally, are you crying?' Connor's high-pitched question startled her. She put a hand to her cheek and was shocked by its wetness. Quickly she wiped her sleeve across her face and sniffed hard.

'No, darling,' she said, trying hard to keep the tremble out of her voice. 'I must have had some dust in my eye.'

But all through dinner, she knew she still looked awful. She could not disguise the dark circles under her eyes, and her nose, despite lashings of face powder, remained pink and shiny. She was unnerved to see that Fletcher didn't look much better. His blue eyes were definitely bloodshot and it appeared he had forgotten to shave or comb his hair. As he sat, quietly munching on his chops, his general demeanour suggested the superhero had been downgraded to something more like the vulnerable Clark Kent.

After the morose meal, Ally took Connor to his bedroom and read him several stories interspersed with frequent cuddles, but eventually, although Ally would have liked to go on reading to him for longer, the boy's eyelids became heavy and drooped over his big brown eyes. She kissed his warm cheek, whispered goodnight and tiptoed out of his room for the last time.

Fletcher was leaning against the veranda rail, his arms crossed over his chest.

'We need to talk.'

'We do?'

There was no answer. Fletcher simply turned on his heel and expected her to follow. Ally knew this was not going to be reconciliation. He was going to lecture her about staying right away from Wallaroo forever. The only hope she could cling to now, was that she would be able to leave in the morning with dignity.

She didn't enjoy feeling like one of the station dogs as she followed at his heels. He led her into his study and, in a gesture disturbingly reminiscent of another occasion, indicated she was to sit in one of the deep cane lounge chairs. Then he inched his length into a chair beside her and began to speak quickly, as if driven by an inner tension.

'In the morning, I will drive you to Townsville and see you safely on a plane south. Once you are back in Melbourne, you will see that I am right. It is for the best.'

'If it's for the best,' she couldn't stop herself from asking, 'why do you look so sad?'

It was true, his face and shoulders sagged and his eyes looked washed out like faded denim, desolate.

She dropped her gaze, aware that he could read too much sympathy in her face.

'Sad?' he barked. 'After all your deception you expect me to be happy?' He swore. 'My God, Ally, how much longer did you intend to keep me in the dark? What if my memory had taken weeks or months to return? Were you ever going to honour me with the truth or did you plan to marry me and then reveal that the bride had duped her husband?'

'No! No, Fletcher!' Ally shouted her defence so loudly she frightened herself. She dropped her voice to a milder tone. 'No, Fletcher, you've got it wrong. I certainly didn't ever plan to trick you into marriage.' She reached out to touch his arm in a gesture of apology—the first time she had voluntarily touched him since they'd returned.

'Then what exactly was the plan?' He sat very still, not moving the arm she touched.

'I just wanted to prove to you that even though I'm a city girl, I can live in the bush and, I'd like to think that, given some time, I could have actually been of some use.' Ally was unable to keep the deep emotion out of her voice. But she saw Fletcher's face harden and she quickly withdrew her hand. He sat staring at the place on his thick forearm where her hand had rested as if she had left a brand.

At the sight of his pensive stare, a tiny quiver of hope tweaked her mouth into a tight smile. 'You see, I used to think you loved me—and, um—that you were just worried about me giving up my career.'

Fletcher stood up then, shaking his head, towering over her. Even now, when there was no sense to it, she couldn't stop her eyes from drinking in the full measure of his physical attractiveness. He had no right to look so sexy when he wasn't even trying. He raked his hand through his hair and gave a bitter laugh. 'That's exactly where you're so mistaken. Even if I—even if I was madly in love with you, love is just not enough for a marriage to work in the outback.'

Ally sat, staring up at him, totally stunned. For several moments she sat completely still and silent, digesting this new information. 'How can you be so sure that love isn't enough?'

He gave her a strange look. 'I've had the very best of evidence—personal experience.'

Her brow wrinkled. 'You—you've been married before?' She worried her bottom lip with her teeth.

'No, no, nothing like that. But my mother—oh, hell!'

His mother! Ally realised then that Fletcher had never elaborated on why his mother lived overseas. She knew his father had died some years ago and she had always assumed that his mother had left after that.

He thrust his hands deep into the pockets of his jeans so that they were stretched tight across his muscular thighs. 'My parents' marriage didn't work for exactly the same reasons that we wouldn't make a go of it.' He paused and took a deep breath, which escaped again as a loud sigh. He sat down again and leaned forward, resting his elbows on his knees, his hands hanging loosely in front of him. His voice, when he spoke again, came out rough and ragged as the confession was torn from his throat. 'My mother left us when I was four.'

'Oh.' Her mouth stayed poised in the shape of an O. Fletcher had only been a little boy like Connor when he lost his mother, too. 'I'm sorry,' she whispered.

'She couldn't take it anymore. Said the bush was stifling her.' The edge of bitterness in his tone was very clear. 'She went back to the city where she had grown up, where she lived an exciting, glittering life. She was a brilliant artist. Just like you, Ally, only she was a musician—a concert pianist. At first she was willing to give up her career, but...'

He paused and Ally didn't interrupt, although protests were rising readily to her lips.

'She really loved my father,' he said softly. 'I'm sure from what people tell me that she was quite besotted with him when they were first married, but...' He swept a hand to the far windows and the moonlit paddocks beyond and shook his head. 'Eventually the bush life took its toll, wore her down...' His tired blue eyes rested on her sadly. 'I've come to realise that the only kind of woman who can take it—this life—is one who's grown up in the bush. One who knows what to expect. I'm sure far too many marriages fall apart because people think they can change—either themselves or their partners.'

Ally couldn't contain herself any longer. Her fighting spirit was simmering fit to boil. 'For goodness' sake, Fletcher, I'm sorry about your mother. Truly sorry. But you can't use that as your sole reason for sending me away. How on earth do you think all the pioneer women who first settled these places coped? They all came from towns and cities. And they put up with conditions a lot worse than this.' She threw her arms wide to take in the comfortably furnished room, the beautiful paintings and the latest technology.

'They were obviously built very tough,' Fletcher tossed back, his eyes raking over Ally's slender frame, inferring that it would never stand the test. 'And they weren't artists, Ally, like my mother and you. They were battlers. Don't forget, my own personal experience has taught me a much more meaningful lesson than some outback folklore. I was a very lonely little boy, without my mother. But my father! Even at my young age, I sensed the change in him. He was a broken man. Oh, he carried on here, but he was alone, very hard and very bitter. He died when I was still at university... I believe his heart had been broken for all those years.'

He picked up the pastoral management textbook lying open on the desk beside him, shut it and placed it back on a shelf. The room was totally silent except for the slow swirl of an overhead fan. 'Mine wasn't a happy childhood. If it hadn't been for my uncle, Lucette's father, and Ned and Mary Harrison...if I hadn't loved the land, the mustering, the life with the stockmen, the peace of the bush.... You see, Ally, you have to love the life, not just the man. There's more to marriage than love-making, unfortunately.'

Desperately, she shook her head at him, the dark curtain of her hair falling across her face. 'Of course there is,' she said, pushing the hair back to tuck it behind one ear in a manner that held his complete attention. 'I understand that marriage requires a great deal of commitment...'

He leant forward and grabbed her hand, gripping it fiercely.

She tried to ignore the effect of his fingers closing round her wrist and kept talking. 'I do love the bush life. I'm going to really miss it! I'm sorry your mother didn't like it here, Fletch, but I do happen to like it very much. I really do.'

His thumb was caressing the back of her hand as he gazed at the floor thoughtfully. She couldn't be sure that he was listening.

'Who was your mother, Fletcher? What was—or should I say—is her name?'

'Oh, she's very well known,' Fletcher replied. 'She is Vivienne Reynaud.'

Ally gasped. 'The French pianist who brought out that wonderful Ravel CD last year?' Suddenly the conflicting images of Fletcher, outback cattleman, and Fletcher, classical musician, slotted into place.

Fletcher's eyebrows rose in surprise then he frowned again. 'Exactly. After she left us her career was more glittering and successful than ever before.'

'How—how did your parents meet?'

'In Paris. My father was over there on a holiday. He went to a concert and fell in love with the beautiful young woman on stage.' His grim facade broke down then and he fixed Ally with a rueful grin. 'Sound familiar?'

It did and perhaps from his perspective there was a weird kind of logic to his thinking.

'You're worried about history repeating itself?'

'It's a pattern as old as time itself.'

'But when Vivienne Reynaud, your mother, came to Wallaroo Downs, she had only ever lived in Europe before?'

'Yes,' Fletcher agreed.

'She grew up in…Paris, perhaps?'

'Yes, she did.'

She glanced quickly at Fletcher's face, but read no

sudden understanding there, so she pressed on. 'Paris is very different from Melbourne...'

'Of course, Ally, but...'

This time there was going to be no buts. Ally allowed herself the luxury of giving full vent to her feelings. She snatched her hand away from his and jumped up, confronting him with as much physical advantage as her small frame would allow.

'Do you mean to tell me that you're comparing me—an Australian girl who's spent heaps of time in the outback—who knew exactly what she was coming to—with a woman from *Paris?*'

She flounced away across the room, too upset for words. This was what had been at the heart of all her sorrow and disappointment. How dense was this man she'd once credited with intelligence as well as a body to die for?

Fletcher was clearly angry, too. She could read the signs—the dangerously hooded eyes, the colour spreading along his cheekbones, the compression of his lips.

'Of course, I didn't make direct comparisons,' he ground out. 'But just because you know a little bit more about the bush than a Parisian, doesn't mean that you won't eventually get bored. The novelty will wear off, Ally. And when the spell fades, Alexandra Fraser will want to return to the glamour of fashion again.'

Ally shrugged. 'And if she does, she will do it from here, designing clothes for women in North Queensland to wear to balls and parties, or sending designs south via your computer.'

Fletcher shook his head, his eyes belying his words by roving hungrily over her as she stood before him. 'It's a pretty little fantasy, Ally, but that's all it is. A totally unrealistic dream.'

Ally bent forward and took his stubbled face in her

hands. Her heart beating wildly, she forced her voice to stay calm as she said, huskily, 'How about a little dose of reality therapy, Fletcher? Why don't you say all this again after you kiss me?'

'Ally.' Fletcher said her name pleadingly, his own voice shaking.

She kissed his lips, lightly but lingeringly. He sat there stiffly as if hypnotised. Her hands slipped under his denim shirt, and she caressed his hair-matted chest, all the while kissing him, not giving him a chance to speak, only to feel.

He gave a deep, shuddering groan and she began to undo the buttons on his shirt. Burying her face in his chest, she tasted the salty tang of his skin.

'Ally, we mustn't, Ally—'

But she went on kissing and caressing him and then she leant closer to whisper against his cheek. 'Say good-bye to me properly, Fletcher. One last time.'

'No. You don't understand.'

'I do. I promise I won't beg you to keep me, or anything like that. Make love to me, please, Fletcher.'

But he held her hands still in his and forced her to listen.

'Don't you see, Ally. I would be the one begging you to stay.'

'You would? Well that's all right then, isn't it?' Ally wriggled provocatively on his lap, guiltily aware of his arousal.

'Damn you, no, Ally, it's not.' Fletcher stood up abruptly, forcing Ally to slide to a crumpled heap on the floor. He bent to help her up, but she slapped his hand away in frustration. Humiliated, she struggled to her feet, her knees almost buckling beneath her.

'This is ridiculous,' she fumed. 'You know what's the matter with you? You're a coward! You're scared of admitting that you're in love with me. And you're terrified of risking failure. How do you think the settlers made a go of the outback in the first place if they didn't take risks? They squared up to face failure year in, year out, and they faced it courageously.'

She paused to take a great, gulping breath and then rushed on. 'I love you, Fletcher Hardy, for better and for worse, unfortunately! But I sure as eggs don't admire you!' And she rushed blindly out of the room.

CHAPTER ELEVEN

As SHE left the Lygon Street coffee shop, Ally pulled up her collar to keep out the chill Melbourne air. Gusts of wind were blowing scraps of paper about her legs as she walked. Only a very few people were hardy enough to sit at tables on the pavement on this dull, depressing afternoon.

She had been dreading having to tell Lucette about the monumental failure of their plans. But Fletcher's cousin had been an empathetic listener. It had been Lucette's idea to meet in her favourite coffee shop, where they could enjoy delicious coffee and cakes as well as the cosily elegant decor.

'It's all so transparent now,' Ally had confessed. 'As far as Fletcher was concerned, our romance was simply a fling. A careless fling! Fun while it lasted—nothing more. I'm a sophisticated city girl. I'm supposed to understand that. Instead I went running after him like some annoying little lovesick schoolgirl.'

Lucette had made appropriate noises as Ally poured out her misery.

'And then I made it ten times worse by brazenly throwing myself at him, and when he lost his memory, I started telling him barefaced lies. No wonder he was so furious with me. No wonder he insisted I leave!'

'The accident certainly complicated things,' agreed Lucette.

'Oh, it only delayed the inevitable.' Ally was sure of that now. That final dumping from Fletcher's lap to the hard floor, followed by the embittered, tense journey to

173

Townsville airport the next morning, had at last brought her to her senses. 'Lucette, you have every right to tell me "I told you so,"' she admitted as she toyed with her cake fork, pushing cherry rum torte around on her plate.

Her friend shook her head. 'Men can be so dumb sometimes, can't they? I think they're born with this in-built conviction that they are right. Have you ever noticed how often they listen to the opinions of another man before they'd listen to a woman?'

Ally nodded. 'But the experience of Fletcher's mother leaving him when he was still so little had a drastic impact, didn't it?'

'It certainly did,' agreed Lucette, 'but you know, Ally, a couple of years ago I visited Aunt Vivienne in Paris and she told me that if Fletcher's dad had tried to get her back she would have come. But she was too proud to come uninvited and Uncle Andrew was too stubborn and too jolly proud to go begging. So they both stayed alone and miserable.'

'That's terrible,' cried Ally. 'Does Fletcher know that?'

Lucette's blue eyes had darted to her coffee cup before she offered an evasive, 'I—I'm not sure.'

'It wouldn't make any difference,' Ally sighed. 'He's obviously inherited stubborn genes from both his parents. So he's doubly pig-headed.'

'Perhaps,' replied Lucette gently. 'Oh, Ally, you poor thing, you're not even enjoying your coffee and cake. Can't you drown your sorrows in a few hundred calories?'

Ally smiled. 'I do appreciate your invitation,' she said. 'This is the first time I've been out of the apartment in the three days since I got back. I wouldn't even admit to my sister just how silly I've been. You're the only person I can talk to about this.'

As she headed for home, Ally was miserably conscious of just how cold and grey and dreary Melbourne could be even in December after the bright sunshine of the tropical outback. Men and women, dressed alike in sombre, dark business suits hurried on and off trams, their pale faces tense and strained. There were no smiles, no one strolling along looking relaxed.

She wondered how many of them had ever seen a platypus in the wild.

They wouldn't care—wouldn't give it a thought, she decided. Until recently, she was like them. Focused on the hectic world of business. Too busy, too ambitious and too self-centred to imagine there was any other satisfying way to live. Now she doubted this city life could satisfy her anymore. Her misery hurt so badly. A deep, heavy pain was lodged permanently in her chest.

She called in at the mini-mart on the corner of her block. She should force herself to make a proper meal this evening. Spicy vegetarian pasta was what she felt like, she decided. She would most definitely avoid beef. She would probably never eat beef again.

It would only remind her of what a fool she had been.

She carried her purchases the last half block to her apartment, trying to psych herself into feeling enthusiastic about preparing a tasty meal. Perhaps she should open a bottle of wine, as a kind of celebration of her entry back into the real world.

Except of course, that she didn't feel celebratory at all.

At least she had kept up the rental on her apartment. A home was something to be grateful for. As she neared her building, a delivery van pulled out of the driveway. We Deliver Anything Anywhere the painted advertisement on its doors claimed. She wondered which of her lucky neighbours had received the delivery. A purchase? A surprise gift?

A final, sudden gust of wind sent her hurrying into the foyer, glad of shelter again.

'Ally, thank heavens you're back.' Mr. and Mrs. Rilke, who shared her floor, were waiting together by the lift. They'd always reminded Ally of a pair of garden gnomes—small, round-faced, with rimless spectacles, they were the most physically alike couple she'd ever encountered.

'What's the problem?' Ally asked.

'Well, dear,' Mrs. Rilke began, 'we're having a bit of trouble getting into our apartment.'

'Have you lost your key?' Ally asked.

'No, dear. It's just that there are all these things blocking the hallway.'

'Purple things,' added Mr. Rilke impatiently. 'We were about to call the caretaker.'

'Purple things?' Ally managed to ask above the sudden violent fluttering of her heart. 'How, how strange.'

'They're for you,' continued Mrs. Rilke. 'I hope you don't mind, dear, but we read some of the cards.'

'So if you'll come on up, we'll help you get them into your apartment, so that we can find our way to our front door,' Mr. Rilke demanded.

'Of course,' whispered Ally, feeling dizzy as her body surged with a dozen different emotions at once.

What could this mean? She leant against the cool metal wall of the lift as they shot to the sixth floor. All she could think was this had something to do with Fletcher, but what or why or how was beyond her. She felt sick.

The lift doors lurched open to reveal a purple spectacle.

'Oh, my!'

The narrow hallway was packed with purple. Pots of purple petunias, vases of purple irises, hydrangeas, pansies and orchids—huge balloons shaped like purple fish floated near the ceiling, while enormous bunches of balloons were tied to an arch suspiciously like one of Lucette's designs. There were purple chocolate boxes, a purple teddy bear and on a small round table in the middle of it all, an enormous heart-shaped bowl of purple passionfruit.

Stupefied, breathless, Ally stared around her, her heartbeat roaring in her ears.

She was dimly aware of the lift doors closing behind her.

'I—I'll just find my key. I'm sorry about this,' she stammered.

'It's mighty weird,' commented Mr. Rilke, shaking his grey head. 'Some people have more money than sense.'

'George,' admonished his wife. 'You keep your opinions to yourself. I think it's romantic.'

'Humph,' muttered her husband.

'OK. I've got the door open,' called Ally. 'Now that archway's the main problem. We'll need to take the balloons off before we can get it through the door.' She had no idea how she managed to think of practical solutions to their dilemma while her heart was pounding fit to burst. With shaking hands she began to untie a cluster of balloons.

Then together with Mr. Rilke, she began to manoeuvre the arch through her doorway.

The lift doors opened with a faint ping.

'Looks like you need a hand,' a familiar deep voice sounded. Ally spun round to see Fletcher stepping through the lift doors, his tall frame almost filling the little remaining space. The Rilkes looked up at him with round, curious eyes. Fletcher scratched his head as he looked at the confusion in the hallway.

'This place is a little smaller than I remembered,' he

offered with a smile and a shrug. 'But hold on, I'll get it cleared in a jiffy.

'What—what are you doing here?' Ally gasped.

'Shopping,' he said with a grin as he took the arch from her and guided it through the doorway with infuriating ease.

'No, I mean it. What are you really doing here?' Ally followed him, a pot plant in each hand. Why was she having so much trouble breathing, speaking and moving?

'Now...' He paused and flashed her one of his trademark grins. 'I think you've stolen my lines. If I remember rightly, a whole lot of trouble started when I asked you those exact questions when you came to Wallaroo.'

Ally noticed the Rilkes standing wide-eyed in the middle of her lounge room with armfuls of purple objects.

'Oh, thank you so much.' She managed to smile at them both. 'Just put those things anywhere you can find a place. The floor will be fine. Is the hallway clear yet?'

'Enough for us to get to our door,' said Mr. Rilke sternly. 'My dear,' he added, eyeing Fletcher up and down with cold suspicion, 'just remember we are right next door if you need help.'

'Oh, yes. Thank you so much. I'm sorry about the— the clutter,' she said as she walked with them to her door.

After Fletcher gathered up the final items and brought them into her lounge room, Ally closed her door and then leant against it, grateful to have something to hold her up.

'What's going on, Fletcher?'

He stood in the middle of her room looking wonderful. His thick, black hair needed cutting and was curling over the top of his cream cable-knit sweater and his cheekbones seemed to stand out more than she remembered.

And he looked tired.

A purple fish floated between them. 'I—I've got something to tell you.'

The bottom suddenly dropped out of her stomach. What on earth could he mean? He looked as nervous and uncertain as he had on the night they first met.

She felt all the colour drain from her face. 'Connor, is he all right?'

'Yes, Ally. Connor's fine. Mary and Ned are spoiling him rotten. But he's missing you.'

That news at least brought a welcoming flood of relief, but the odd tone in his voice bothered her—something edgy and defensive that she couldn't quite put her finger on. And his eyes—what was it about his eyes? Why was he looking at her like that? Something about his expression made her stomach tighten alarmingly.

His throat worked. 'Connor's not the only one who's missed you, Ally. I've come to take you back.'

'What?' she asked after a long moment.

'I know this sounds crazy…'

Ally just stared at him, blinking rapidly, hating the ridiculous tears that stung her eyes. 'You want me to come back to Wallaroo?'

He squared his shoulders. 'I'm asking you to forgive me. No, damn it. Well, yes, I am, but, Ally, I want more than that. I want you to marry me.' He spoke quickly, nervously.

Ally felt dizzy.

Fletcher walked towards where she stood stiffly against the door. 'I've been a fool,' he whispered, and lifted a gentle finger to trail down one tear-stained cheek.

'But you never meant to get involved,' she protested. 'I—I forced myself on you. You were right. I'm…'

'Ally.' He placed the finger firmly over her babbling mouth. 'Be quiet.'

She looked up at him as he leant closer; so close she

could see each individual eyelash around his deep blue eyes. She stood there ramrod-stiff while her eyes searched his face wildly for a clue to this behaviour. Her mind seemed to have turned to cotton wool. Nothing made sense.

'Sweetheart, listen to me carefully, please. Admitting even once that I've been a total idiot doesn't come easily.'

Her eyes widened further and her heart began to pick up pace again. Behind him all she could see were splashes of purple.

'I know I had a bang on the head, but that's not really enough of an excuse for the way I treated you.' He held her shoulders in both hands, his thumbs outlining her collarbone. 'Everything you said the other night is true, Ally. I have been an absolute coward. I've let one little childhood fear about my parents hold me back from reaching for—for the ultimate happiness.'

Perhaps she was dreaming. Had she suffered a caffeine overdose from her afternoon with Lucette?

Fletcher dipped his head towards her and his lips brushed hers, a feather-light touch, sweet and tender. She shivered.

He smiled wryly. 'My poor, brave little Ally. You've taken so many risks for me. You put absolutely everything on the line. You gave up your career, sacrificed your pride. How can I ever thank you?'

She was beginning to think of some pretty audacious ways, but for the moment, she stayed quiet and still, not daring to prick the fragile bubble of hope that was forming somewhere deep inside.

'As soon as I put you on that plane I knew I'd made the most terrible, terrible mistake.'

Was she really hearing this?

'I should have known that we can never be certain

about the future. Somehow, I'd convinced myself that saying no to what I really wanted was the courageous option. You, you sweet, gutsy little angel, showed me just how off-track I was. I was fooling myself and I was trying to fool you.'

He grinned then, a shy, uncertain offering. 'Can you forgive me?'

She felt her mouth begin to split into a wide answering grin. 'I might be able to,' she whispered, looking at him, her eyes bright.

Suddenly his arms were around her, lifting her up, pulling her tightly against him. His mouth closed over hers, sealing her to him and his hands ran over her desperately, as if wanting to feel all of her at once. His touch made her feel weak and shivery and melting inside.

He drew back to gaze at her, his eyes glinting with something remarkably moist. 'Thank God, you bullied me,' he sighed at last. One hand stroked her hair as she looked up at him smiling broadly. 'Thank God, you wouldn't give up,' he said, his eyes gleaming as they took in every detail. It was as if he were examining a very, very precious gift.

'Fletcher,' she murmured, her voice low and husky, treasuring the name as it left her lips. With a happy sigh, she brought his head down to hers for another longer kiss.

'Marry me, Ally. Please marry me. If you hate the bush, we'll leave together. We'll make a new life somewhere else, but I've got to have you. I can't bear to let you go.'

'Idiot,' Ally laughed as she kissed him gently on the nose. 'I'm not going to want to go anywhere else. You're there. That's all I want.' She nibbled his chin playfully with her neat white teeth, relishing the masculine texture, then ran happy kisses over his neck. 'You're all I've ever wanted. I happen to love you.'

He crushed her to him, as if afraid she would suddenly disappear.

'Let's go somewhere more comfortable,' she murmured, leading the way out of the lounge room.

In her bedroom, they lay together for a moment, lost in each other's arms, savouring the moment, wanting to make it a lasting memory. He raised his head and smiled down at her. 'I really didn't want you to have to give everything up. You are such a clever designer.'

Ally pushed him gently away and fixed him with a stern glare. 'Fletcher, let me get this into your thick head for the last time. I want you. Nothing else. I love you more than catwalks and luxury fabrics. I love you more than magazine coverage. I'm not giving anything up. I'm getting what I want.' She touched his cheek and saw him tremble. 'You're all I've wanted ever since I met you. Hey, I'm getting the most gorgeous guy in Australia. And, as a bonus—I—I think he loves me.'

'Think? Ally, rest assured. I don't deserve you, but I love you.' He kissed her. 'I love you.' Then he kissed her again.

Ally kissed him back and it was the longest time before they drew apart.

'How did we end up on my bed?' she murmured seductively as she began to unbutton his shirt.

He kissed her again, a long, slow, sensuous kiss this time and it was dreadful when he finally broke away to ask huskily, 'Hold on a minute, little minx, you haven't answered my question yet.'

'I haven't? What question was that?' Her eyes twinkled wickedly as her hands reached his belt buckle.

'I've asked you to make an honest man of me. You haven't said you'll marry me.'

'I haven't said?' Ally cried. 'Fletcher, my darling, that's why I came to Wallaroo Downs. You couldn't doubt that I want to marry you. I've practically begged. You just want to hear me say yes?'

With a growl of pleasure, Fletcher rolled her across the bed, so that his entire weight was pinning her with delicious strength to the mattress. 'Yes, Alexandra Fraser. I want—I need to hear you say yes.'

She eyed him. 'Yes, Fletcher Hardy, my dearest man. Of course I'll marry you.' She offered him her lips, which he took in another deep, lingering kiss and from which she only just dragged herself away. 'But I have a special request.'

'Anything, my sweet.'

'I want the wedding to be at Wallaroo. I want all my friends to come and see my man and his land.'

'It's a deal,' he whispered.

EPILOGUE

AS HIS horse slowed to a trot, Fletcher Hardy lowered his hat so that it shaded his eyes from the glaring afternoon sun. That was better. Now as his mount carried him up from the creek, he could have an uninterrupted view across the home paddock towards the homestead.

It always gave him great satisfaction to see his home come into view at the end of a long, hot day in the saddle. Circled by the huge shade trees, its long rambling roofline fringed by the deep verandas always induced a welcome sense of calm. He squinted, trying to make out the shapes on the veranda. There was little Sarah, hopping and skipping in time to a definite rhythm. Last week, Ally had taught her how to work the tape recorder, so that she could play her favourite music and dance to her heart's delight whenever she chose.

At three, their dark-haired, blue-eyed daughter was already showing a noticeably artistic bent, but she was far too bossy. He felt sorry for the new baby when it arrived in two months' time. With Sarah for a big sister, it would have to come out fighting.

He could see Ally now, walking along the veranda— to call Sarah in for her bath, most likely. He felt his smile widen as he watched his wife's blossoming figure trundle along. He loved her more than ever when she was pregnant. She positively glowed with good health and happiness as if the baby she nurtured was a health tonic.

He had been so worried the first time, when their son Fraser was born. But Ally had never been more serene. A week before the due date, she asked him to drive her into Charters Towers and two days later, produced a fat, bouncing boy—a wonderful companion for Connor.

By the time he reached the stables, his boys, Connor and Fraser, were already there, mucking out their horses' stalls. It was their favourite haunt. At ten, Connor was a tall, strong boy who was as easygoing and good-natured as ever. Fletcher had always felt his godson was a great role model for his own son and they would all miss him badly when he left after Christmas for the boarding school Fletcher and Jock Lawrence had attended.

He stabled the horse and, with a nod to the boys, moved off to hang the saddle away in the tack room.

'I thought I might find you in here.' Ally's lilting voice reached him as she crossed the old brick floor to greet her husband. Standing on tiptoe to kiss him, she wound her cool arms around his neck.

'Mmm,' murmured Fletcher, nibbling her neck. 'You smell wonderful, delicious.'

Ally laughed. 'You smell—well like a man who's been in the saddle since dawn. Dusty but nice.'

Fletcher growled. 'Be careful, wife, there are no children in sight and I haven't yet made love to you in here.'

'Well, there aren't many places left we haven't tried,' rejoined Ally with a wicked gleam in her eye. 'But,' she added, punching him playfully, 'Mary has dinner almost ready and your tribe will be ravenous as always.'

'And their mother is ravishing.' Fletcher smiled, holding her at arm's length to take a good look at his wife. Her dark hair was twisted into a fetching knot at the nape of her neck and she was dressed in a soft smock that leant violet tints to her clear eyes, now shining with love. Her cheeks were lightly flushed and she was breathtakingly beautiful.

'Thank goodness you bullied me into marriage,' he said softly as he had a hundred other times, lifting a fine strand of hair and tucking it behind her ear. 'I love you, Ally Hardy.'

Ally sighed happily, drawing close to her husband again, clearly revelling in the joy of his strong arms around her. He saw her beautiful smile drawing up the corners of her mouth. 'I love you back,' she murmured.

'Now, no more talk. I'm going to kiss you before these children...'

He didn't finish the sentence. Ally lifted her face to his and whatever he was going to say seemed a precious waste of time.

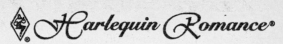
Harlequin Romance®

We're proud to announce the "birth" of a brand-new series full of babies, bachelors and happy-ever-afters: ***Daddy Boom***. Meet gorgeous heroes who are about to discover that there's a first time for everything—even fatherhood!

We'll be bringing you one deliciously cute ***Daddy Boom*** title every other month in 1999. Books in this series are:

February 1999 **BRANNIGAN'S BABY**
Grace Green
April 1999 **DADDY AND DAUGHTERS**
Barbara McMahon
June 1999 **THE DADDY DILEMMA**
Kate Denton
August 1999 **OUTBACK WIFE AND MOTHER**
Barbara Hannay
October 1999 **THE TYCOON'S BABY**
Leigh Michaels
December 1999 **A HUSBAND FOR CHRISTMAS**
Emma Richmond

Who says bachelors and babies don't mix?

Available wherever Harlequin books are sold.

HARLEQUIN®
Makes any time special.™

If you enjoyed what you just read,
then we've got an offer you can't resist!

Take 2 bestselling love stories FREE!

Plus get a FREE surprise gift!

Clip this page and mail it to Harlequin Reader Service®

IN U.S.A.	IN CANADA
3010 Walden Ave.	P.O. Box 609
P.O. Box 1867	Fort Erie, Ontario
Buffalo, N.Y. 14240-1867	L2A 5X3

YES! Please send me 2 free Harlequin Romance® novels and my free surprise gift. Then send me 4 brand-new novels every month, which I will receive months before they're available in stores. In the U.S.A., bill me at the bargain price of $2.90 plus 25¢ delivery per book and applicable sales tax, if any*. In Canada, bill me at the bargain price of $3.34 plus 25¢ delivery per book and applicable taxes**. That's the complete price and a savings of over 10% off the cover prices—what a great deal! I understand that accepting the 2 free books and gift places me under no obligation ever to buy any books. I can always return a shipment and cancel at any time. Even if I never buy another book from Harlequin, the 2 free books and gift are mine to keep forever. So why not take us up on our invitation. You'll be glad you did!

116 HEN CNEP
316 HEN CNEQ

Name	(PLEASE PRINT)	
Address	Apt.#	
City	State/Prov.	Zip/Postal Code

* Terms and prices subject to change without notice. Sales tax applicable in N.Y.
** Canadian residents will be charged applicable provincial taxes and GST.
   All orders subject to approval. Offer limited to one per household.
® are registered trademarks of Harlequin Enterprises Limited.

HROM99   ©1998 Harlequin Enterprises Limited

ℋarlequin Romance®

brings you four very special weddings to remember in our new series:

WHITE WEDDINGS

True love is worth waiting for....

Look out for the following titles by some of your favorite authors:

August 1999—SHOTGUN BRIDEGROOM #3564
Day Leclaire
Everyone is determined to protect Annie's good name and ensure that bad boy Sam's seduction attempts don't end in the bedroom—but begin with a wedding!

September 1999—A WEDDING WORTH WAITING FOR #3569
Jessica Steele
Karrie was smitten by boss Farne Maitland. But she was determined to be a virgin bride. There was only one solution: marry and quickly!

October 1999—MARRYING MR. RIGHT #3573
Carolyn Greene
Greg was wrongly arrested on his wedding night for something he didn't do! Now he's about to reclaim his virgin bride when he discovers Christina's intention to marry someone else....

November 1999—AN INNOCENT BRIDE #3577
Betty Neels
Katrina didn't know it yet but Simon Glenville, the wonderful doctor who'd cared for her sick aunt, was in love with her. When the time was right, he was going to propose....

Available wherever Harlequin books are sold.

HARLEQUIN®
Makes any time special.™

Look us up on-line at: http://www.romance.net

HRWW

Coming Next Month

#3579 LONG-LOST BRIDE Day Leclaire
Chaz found himself proposing to a beautiful mystery woman at the masked ball. She turned out to be Shayne—the woman he'd once loved more than life itself. They both needed to marry—but could Chaz ever truly forgive his long-lost bride?

Fairytale Weddings: The Fairytale Weddings Ball: come single, leave wed!

#3580 A HUSBAND FOR CHRISTMAS Emma Richmond
Gellis had begun to assume that Sebastien Fourcard had left her for another woman, when he returned—with amnesia! He couldn't remember loving Gellis, but he wanted to stay for the sake of their son. Gellis wanted his love—but not just for Christmas....

Daddy Boom: Who says bachelors and babies don't mix?

#3581 KISSING SANTA Jessica Hart
Amanda had to get Blair McAllister to sell his home to her company. But her plan to get close to him by taking the job of nanny to his three children backfired when she fell in love! Work forgotten, now all Amanda wanted was Blair—under the mistletoe....

#3582 RESOLUTION: MARRIAGE Patricia Knoll
Garrett Blackhawk is acting as if he never wrote to end his relationship with Mary Jane. He still wants her as his wife! Mary Jane is tempted, but forced to keep her distance. At least, until she's ready to share her secret—that her eldest daughter is also his!

Marriage Ties: The four Kelleher women, bound together by family and love